The Rinaldi Ring

Also by Jenny Nimmo

Jenny Nimmo

The Rinaldi Ring

Jenny Nimmo

EGMONT

For Miriam and Gwen
without whom this book would not have been written.

EGMONT
We bring stories to life

First published in Great Britain 1999
Reissued 2005
by Egmont Books Ltd
239 Kensington High Street
London W8 6SA

Text copyright © Jenny Nimmo 1999
Cover illustration copyright © Sharon Chai 2005

The moral rights of the author and illustrator have been asserted.

ISBN 1 4052 1141 5

1 3 5 7 9 10 8 6 4 2

A CIP catalogue record for this title is available from the British Library

Typeset by Avon DataSet Ltd, Bidford on Avon
Printed and bound in Great Britain by the CPI Group

CONTENTS

1

The crime

One day Eliot and his mother took a road they had been warned against. It was blistering in town, the sun burned relentlessly and Florida heat shimmered on the tarmac. Lily Latimer had tender, ivory skin. She turned into a narrow tree-lined road, and Eliot followed.

Where the shadows thinned, flowers brightened the verge and butterflies danced in pools of dazzling colour. Eliot knew it was a dangerous place. His father had told them not to stray. Trouble hid in corners, in alleys and rough, shady roads. Only last week a tourist had been mugged and badly wounded. Eliot was twelve and curious about danger. He longed to test his courage, but as Lily wandered further down the empty road, he felt a small flicker of doubt and found himself saying, 'Mum, I think we should go back.'

'Let me cool down, honey.' His mother walked on. 'Will you look at that!' She nodded at a butterfly, its ruby wings spread against white petals. It flew off as two youths stepped into the road ahead. Eliot moved closer to his mother and the taller boy said, 'Purse, lady!'

Lily had promised her husband that if threatened with

violence, she would always do whatever was necessary to avoid it. But she was not a meek person and Gilbert Latimer knew she would find it hard to oblige a criminal. 'Life is more precious than possessions,' he said, 'and Eliot and I would never forgive you if, needlessly, you gave yours away.'

Did he know, even then, what would happen?

As the youths strolled closer, Eliot waited for his mother to hand over her bag. It hung by a strap from her shoulder, a small red leather bag with a silver clasp. She seemed unable to let it go. Her fingers closed over the bag and her face took on a stubborn, flinty look.

One of the youths held a blade that caught the sun in a sudden flash.

'Mum!' Eliot tugged her arm. She shook her head.

And then it was over. He was beaten backwards as the bag was ripped from his mother's arm, and he heard a dull thud as his skull hit the pavement. When he got to his feet, Lily was lying very still and her golden hair was threaded with dust. The blood from her heart resembled nothing so much as a dark butterfly, pinned to her blouse.

Eliot screamed and tried to reach for his mother, but someone held him back. A policewoman, her face expressionless, said, 'Don't touch her, honey!' He didn't think to ask her why.

He could recall only brief interludes in the week that followed. He spent most of his time in a hotel apartment, but if you had asked him to describe his surroundings he could not have done it. He remembered tanned policemen, always at the door, his Russian grandmother holding his hand, reading stories like Lily used to when he was very small, and sitting by his bed until he fell asleep. He remembered his window banging in an unexpected breeze, and his father pacing the rooms with ruined, sleepless eyes, never speaking of his wife. Did he blame her? Eliot wondered.

The funeral took place on a sunny hillside with a breathtaking view of the ocean. The graveyard trees were like carved stone, their sparse foliage affording little shade. Eliot, standing between Grandpa and Grandma Morozov, listened to the melodious intoning of the Russian priest but didn't understand him. There was a crush of black-clothed people round the chasm in the ground, their faces glistening in the sun. The coffin was covered in lilies and white roses, and Gilbert Latimer watched stony-faced as a crimson butterfly settled on a wreath.

Another week followed. Eliot's father wound up his business in America and said goodbye to the few people he knew. Eliot stayed in a white clapboard house with Grandpa and Grandma Morozov until his father came to fetch him. 'We'll never come back,' Gilbert told his son, 'never. Grey skies are better than cold hearts.'

Eliot couldn't understand his father. His grandparents didn't have cold hearts. They hugged him tight and sobbed when he left them. Grandpa Morozov gave him a baseball and a brand new leather mitt. 'This *is* America,' he told Eliot. 'Practise well, and one day, when you come back, you might be a champ.' He was proud of being an American, though he still used his new language in an odd, poetic sort of way.

From the car window, Eliot watched them vanish. Two grey-haired people on a flight of steps, forever waving. 'We must come back,' he said to Gilbert, 'for them.'

'Never,' said his father.

Then I'll run away, thought Eliot.

2
The runner

The first time Eliot ran away he got as far as Hyde Park. His father's apartment was less than a mile away so he didn't consider it a serious flight. He sat on a park bench in the rain and went home, soaked through, when the gates were locked. Gilbert was still too remote to be angry. 'Get changed,' he said coldly. 'I suppose you're hungry.'

On the second occasion Eliot spent a night in a school friend's greenhouse. The boy's father discovered him next morning, asleep on a pile of sacking. He was driven home to find his father white-faced and distraught. All night he had been searching London, along with half the police force, so it seemed to Eliot. Astonished by his father's anguish, he promised never to run away again.

Gilbert hired a live-in housekeeper; an efficient, middle-aged woman called Mary Parkin, who cooked without inspiration and had little conversation. Her customary response to Eliot's problems was, 'Oh, dear!' spoken in tones of weary sarcasm. Eliot decided that English hearts were drained of love. He wrote to Grandpa and Grandma Morozov every week, always ending with the fervent wish that he would see them soon.

Six months passed. Gilbert Latimer lost his stormy desolate look, but this was gradually replaced by a vacant indifference that Eliot longed to wipe away. It cannot have affected his father's flair for business, however, for Gilbert was soon a director of a large export firm. He spent several days a month travelling in Eastern Europe, and when he returned from these visits he would describe to Eliot the people he had met, and the exotic-sounding towns where he had passed his time. He even explained a little of the work he was engaged in. Eliot began to look forward to these companionable evenings with his father. And then, one day, he said, 'Mum liked snowy places. D'you remember the big fur hat? D'you remember how she . . .?'

Gilbert got up and walked away. 'Put the past behind you, Eliot,' he said coldly. 'Forget it. Our lives are different now.'

Next day Eliot took the pocket money he had saved and went to the airport by taxi. He couldn't afford the fare to America so he bought a ticket for Glasgow instead. For two nights he managed to evade the police by staying awake at night, hiding in alleys and doorways. By day he would take short naps on park benches. On a visit to the museum he was seduced by the music of a visiting chamber orchestra and, propped against the glass cabinet of a stuffed wildcat, fell into a deep sleep.

He was not fully awake when they pulled him to his feet, and only remembered where he was when he had passed the rows of dead animals, and began to stumble out into fresh air.

'What am I going to do with you?' Gilbert asked when he came to fetch him home. 'What do you want? Tell me, Eliot, because I don't know.'

'I don't know either,' Eliot lied.

It was at this point that Gilbert's cousin, Sophie Piper, stepped in. Gilbert's parents were both dead and as he was an only child he had no other relative to turn to.

Sophie suggested that Eliot come and stay with her. Never mind that the holidays had not begun. She would enrol him in school ready for the next term. A few weeks without lessons wouldn't matter. He must come to Saintbury now. Her daughters Noni and Violet would be delighted.

Gilbert read the letter to his son over breakfast. Eliot listened without enthusiasm. 'Weird name, Noni,' was his only comment.

'Anemone,' his father told him. 'Heaven knows why she's called Noni.'

'Easier,' mumbled Eliot.

'I think it's for the best, don't you?' said his father. 'You'll have company.'

'Girls,' said Eliot.

'Eliot, I didn't want this. I thought we'd be all right, you and me. But it's not working, is it?' Gilbert looked strained, almost embarrassed.

'I guess not.'

His father suddenly stood up, saying, 'Perhaps you'd like to sort some stuff out. Books, things you don't want to leave behind. I'll tell Mary to pack the clothes. You'd better take everything.'

Eliot imagined an empty cupboard, his bedroom stark and tidy, his father utterly alone, and a tide of misgiving washed over him. Their life together had gone badly wrong, but it was ending now and there was nothing he could do to save it.

He spent the day finding the books that Lily had chosen for him; stories from Arabia, Russia and Ancient Greece. His mother had loved myths and tales of enchantment, together they had read them over and again. The pages were crumpled with fingering. It was these books that Eliot packed.

They set off early next morning, and neither of them felt like talking on the journey north. But when they stopped for a snack at a service station, Gilbert said, 'It's a decent town, Saintbury. It was built in the middle ages, in the centre of an ox-bow lake. It's where my parents came from, and I lived there, off and on, for eighteen years.'

Eliot felt a stirring of interest. 'Why've I never been there before?'

'You have,' his father told him. 'When you were five we spent Christmas with the Pipers. They were a merry family. You probably don't remember.'

But he did. Now it came to him. Two girls, one dark the other fair. He remembered their laughter and their constant movement, upstairs, downstairs, into the garden. He hadn't thought of them as separate personalities. They were just 'them'. The girls. And he'd felt left out. He hadn't forgotten that. 'Suppose I change my mind,' he said to Gilbert. 'Suppose I come back with you and promise never to run away again?'

'Oh, Eliot,' his father groaned. 'It's too late now.'

As they passed over the bridge into town, Eliot began to recognise some of the buildings: half-timbered facades, steep, tiled roofs and lofty, ragged chimneys.

They parked at the end of Fly Street and walked to the house. The buildings here were Georgian, tall and elegant. Black palings and rosy brick walls swathed in ivy, swam past Eliot's eyes, and then he saw the house and even before he reached the door, felt the presence behind it. He began to feel breathless and took short, painful gulps of air.

'Eliot?' Gilbert clutched his arm and studied him closely. There was a curiously intense expression in his father's bruised-looking eyes, and for a fleeting moment Eliot sensed that his father knew about the 'presence' in the house.

'I'm OK, Dad,' he said.

But this was not quite true, for when the door opened and he found himself face to face with two half-remembered cousins, he said 'Ah, Snow White and Rose Red, I presume.'

It was not a promising beginning. From their slight and unamused smiles, Eliot judged that he couldn't have said anything worse.

3
The angel

Noni was Rose Red. She was thirteen, a year older than Eliot. Her curly hair was a deep red-brown and her eyes were the same colour. Violet, a year younger, was pale and thin-faced. She had grey-green eyes and hair like yellow silk. They were certainly not a double act now. They had acquired very separate personalities. Noni attacked life as though it were trying to defeat her. She was incapable of being still, her thoughts spilling over in wild exclamations and sudden bursts of furious energy. Violet was grave and calm, the quiet victim of her sister's moods.

The girls didn't resent the sudden addition to their family, but at first Eliot felt like a specimen on a tray, or a mouse watched by cats. He could sense them observing his movements, waiting for signs of disturbance, waiting for him to run away. Eliot decided that he wouldn't satisfy them. He would stick it out.

On his first morning, when Sophie and he were left alone in the kitchen, Sophie said, in a business-like tone, 'Now, Eliot, we'd better have a chat. I shan't try to be a mother, I think it's too late for that. But I'll try and be the next best thing, whatever that is. We're your family and this is your home, and we'll be very sad if you run away. We'll always come and get you, wherever you are. Obviously you need a certain amount of freedom, so I'm going to give you the front-door key and you can come and go as you please. I'm a busy person – committees, that sort of thing. I'm an accountant – part-time – and I work in there!' She indicated, with a nod, the room just across the hall. 'But today is yours, Eliot,' she said warmly. 'I'm going to give you a tour.'

Sophie took him round the girls' favourite haunts, showed him the river and its seven bridges, the park, the tennis courts and the swimming pool. Before they went home she bought a pile of graphic novels, to keep for those moments of idleness when he might find himself dwelling on the past.

They settled into a routine, and whatever it was that had made Eliot afraid of the house on that first day, it allowed him a week of peace before insinuating itself into his life again.

When the girls came home from school Noni would take him down to the tennis courts, or Violet would chuck the baseball at him in the walled back garden. She referred to his mitt as the ape's foot. 'Baseball's a weird game,' she said. 'You can't play it properly here, so why bother to practise?'

'For my Russian-American grandfather,' Eliot told her. 'He thinks it's important.'

'Oh!' Violet looked grave. 'Then it is.'

Noni called their father 'the dentist'. She had always

wanted to use her parents' Christian names, but disliked her father's, which was Donald. Dentist was a compromise. The dentist appeared to find it amusing. He was a quiet, humorous man with thinning fair hair, who still seemed rather surprised to find himself the father of two girls. 'Ah,' he would say on his return from an afternoon's drilling, 'people!' As if he had spent a year in outer space and half-expected his own race to have died out.

Now and again Eliot smiled. Once or twice he laughed. He realised that he was almost happy. And if there was an undercurrent in the house, a sense of something unseen hanging about him, it seemed to welcome rather than resent him, and he was comforted by its presence, as though a guardian angel watched over him. But he suspected that, sooner or later, the angel would break cover and reveal its purpose.

It happened on a chilly afternoon at exactly five o'clock. Sophie and the dentist were out, but the girls were home and Violet had baked a quick-rising sponge cake. Eliot was sitting at the scrubbed kitchen table, savouring the smell of home cooking, when the doorbell went, and he burst out, 'Don't answer it!'

Noni, slicing cake, looked up, surprised by Eliot's sudden vehemence. 'Who's after you, Eliot?' she asked with a sly grin.

Violet said, 'It could be urgent.'

After a short interval the familiar chime came again, shrill but not insistent. Eliot felt his spine grow rigid. Noni went to the door and he followed. A woman, moving away from the house, looked back at them.

'Did you ring?' asked Noni.

The woman turned. 'Yes.' She came to the foot of the stone steps. 'Is Mrs Piper in?'

'No. But she'll be back soon. Can I help?'

'It's the Flower Festival in July. Just a reminder. She likes to help. You've got a lovely garden tucked back there, haven't you?' The woman craned towards the open door, yellowish eyes seeking the garden.

'Mum's pride and joy.' Noni listed the rare plants that Sophie had coaxed into bloom. The woman listened with a fixed, unsmiling expression, while Eliot noted the colourless clothes and coarse grey hair. She seemed not to reflect the light. Something was wrong. His glance was drawn by a force quite outside his will to her right hand – and he saw the ring.

It was an oval pearl set in a bed of tiny sapphires and rubies. The band was gold. Eliot gazed at the ring and it was as though someone else, behind his eyes, recognised it. He was overwhelmed by a desperate yearning, a need to touch the ring.

Without looking at Eliot, the woman pushed her right hand into her pocket. Out of sight. And Eliot knew her as an enemy.

'It's chilly for May,' she said, drawing up her collar with her left hand. She walked away; a tall woman with narrow feet in black, laced shoes, taking long, forceful strides; grey hair unmoving in the sudden breeze. She seemed to set the day on edge.

'Weird.' Noni closed the door. 'But not that weird,'

seeing Eliot's strained, white face. 'She wasn't a ghost. Oh, I'm sorry, Eliot. I didn't mean . . .'

He opened the door again and stepped out.

'Eliot?' Noni said.

He began to run. The woman was still in sight but her pace had quickened. She rounded a corner and vanished. Eliot tore after her and was just in time to see a black door, halfway down the next street, close so quietly, even the click of the latch could not be heard.

Eliot walked down the opposite pavement until he came to the house with the black door. It was a red-brick terraced house, three storeys high, with white-painted window frames, some of them peeling. A polished brass knocker in the shape of a hawk was set a few inches above the number on the door: number seven. The place was almost identical to the other houses in the street. It was not at all remarkable, except for the hushed, smothered feeling that crept across the road to Eliot, almost choking him. Yet he had passed this way before and felt nothing.

The net curtain in a top window moved a fraction and then was still. Eliot knew that he was being watched. As he retraced his steps, an intense feeling of desolation pressed about him, shrouding the street in a haze of unfamiliar light and shadow, even the smell and feel of the air was different. When he reached the Pipers' house he ran up the steps and slammed the door behind him.

Noni swung round as he came into the kitchen. 'What made you take off like that? You weren't upset by . . . by something I said were you?'

Eliot could not explain. Something had driven him after the yellow-eyed woman, but what? 'Have you seen that woman before?' he asked.

'Might have,' Noni said. 'She looked like a hundred others.'

'She did *not*. She was utterly different. Utterly!' Eliot declared.

Violet looked up from her exercise book. 'How different?' she asked.

'Tall, and kinda rigid,' Eliot told her eagerly. 'A sharp nose and yellowy eyes, like a buzzard. And she seemed . . .' he struggled for the right description, 'out of place. Like she didn't belong with real people.'

'Greymark,' Violet said. 'Freya Greymark.' She returned to her book, seeking her place.

Noni was frowning. 'How d'you know?' She was irritated by Violet's flatly delivered information. How did her sister manage to know so much?

'I just know,' said Violet smiling.

'Greymark,' Eliot repeated. 'Freya Greymark. Of course!'

'Of course! Of course!' Noni repeated. 'What d'you mean "of course"?'

'I mean it sounds right,' he said, unable to tell her that the name struck a chord in a part of his mind that seemed to have been hijacked by somebody else. He began to circle the kitchen in long restless strides. 'She wore a ring,' he murmured. 'A special ring, creamy-white, a pearl, soft not sparkling. And old, old, old.'

'Didn't know you were interested in jewellery,' Noni still sounded huffy.

'Please,' begged Eliot. 'I have to know.' Even as he spoke, he was thinking: what's happening? Why should I care?

The front door banged and Noni said, 'Mum will know.'

Sophie swung in, dripping plastic bags. 'Should've taken the car,' she grunted. 'I knew it. Took ages. Food's heavy, specially fruit and veg, weighs a ton!'

'Hardly.' Noni peeled the shopping away from her mother.

'A ton!' Sophie repeated with emphasis. 'Tea?'

Violet, flipping her book page down on to the table, said, 'I'll get it.' She went to the sink and filled the kettle.

'Is the dentist in?' Sophie flung herself into a chair and stretched her legs out before her.

'The dentist isn't in,' Noni told her mother. 'But we had a visitor. A woman like a buzzard, an unreal kind of person,' she glanced at Eliot. 'Violet says it's Freya Greymark.'

'Oh, her,' said Sophie. 'It's the flowers, isn't it? She's always after my sweet rocket. *Hesperis Matronalis*, she calls it. I tell her every year, it only lasts until mid-July. It will be over when the Flower Festival starts. Why can't she be satisfied with roses?'

'She didn't mention anything specific,' Noni said. 'She just wanted to remind you about the Festival.'

'Huh! She'll be back,' said Sophie. 'Last year she persuaded me to give her an armful for the church. But when I went to look at her arrangements, it wasn't there. She'd only used lilies and daisies. So what did she do with my sweet rocket?'

'Eliot's interested in her ring,' Noni said. 'He thinks it's special.'

'Her ring?' Sophie frowned. 'Well, there is a story attached to it. I can't quite remember it, now.'

'Think I'll take a walk,' muttered Eliot. He felt restless. 'I want to see the cygnets.'

They looked at him with a sympathetic interest and he knew they were wondering if tears would flow, down by the river. While he was gazing at the swans would his thoughts be with his mother? Why didn't they ask out loud?

'D'you want to be by yourself?' asked Noni.

'Yeah.' It didn't matter what they thought. He couldn't tell them that he felt compelled to pass the house in Salter Row, the house with a black door and a cold brass hawk. He couldn't explain that, even to himself.

There was a book in the pocket of his anorak, he noticed the slight bulge when he took it from the hall stand. But he thought nothing of it.

When he reached the river the swan and her cygnets were not where he expected them to be. So he began to follow the river walk that almost encircled the town.

He passed three bridges; a splendid stone edifice with buttresses and tall Victorian gas lamps, a narrow iron bridge that led to the carpark and a sturdy concrete construction taking traffic on to the motorway. Eliot did not cross the river until he reached an elegant footbridge to the park, his favourite. It was painted white and, on windy days, swung gently like a ship at sea. When he was halfway across he leaned on the railing and gazed into the dark water. There was only a light breeze and the bridge refused to swing for him.

The park was deserted except for a lone cyclist pedalling like fury. Everyone had rushed home for tea. Eliot felt in his pocket and took out the book. It was not his. Someone must have mistaken his anorak for theirs. 'Poetry,' he said and would have shoved it back, but the book fell open and a title caught his eye. 'But I was looking at the permanent stars.'

Eliot began to read.

It was the work of Wilfred Owen, someone Eliot had never heard of. And the poems told of a war he knew nothing about. It was long ago and empty of the things that usually excited Eliot: tanks, helicopters and screaming jets. The words described soldiers' faces, their limbs and their souls. They seemed very young. Boys, a few years older than he was, brave and sorrowful. He did not understand the meaning of every line, but a message reached him of terrible despair. And although his mother had no place in the world of dead and dying soldiers, he thought of her.

He sat on a bench beneath a willow tree while the pale blue light of dusk began to fill the park. And he could feel a watchfulness, very close, and wondered if the angel from the house had followed him. There was a strange fragrance in the air – like flowers. He did not notice it was growing cold until the church clock began to chime. How many times? Six or seven?

A crowd of ducks suddenly skimmed over the water and took off, calling to each other in raucous, agitated voices. Eliot ran to the bridge to see what had disturbed them. But nothing ruffled the water and the river was quiet. He ascended the planked slope up to the bridge and then, feeling a light drizzle on his face, began to run. He didn't stop until he reached Salter Row. When he passed the black door he heard the faint tap of footsteps in his wake. He glanced back swiftly, but there was no one there. He crossed the road and went right up to the black door of number seven. He stared intently at the brass hawk, wanting to touch it, but drew back and hastened down the street, puzzled by his behaviour. And then someone else used the knocker. It rang out quite clearly, brass on brass. It could have been nothing else, and yet there was no one on the step of number seven. The street was deserted except for two women at the far end, chatting under the branches of a chestnut tree. Again he was mystified by the scent of unseen flowers.

Sophie gave him a quick smile when he came in. 'Getting to know your way about, Eliot?' she asked.

He mumbled, 'Yeah.'

The dentist was reading a newspaper at the kitchen table. He rustled the pages and beamed at Eliot. 'Good!' he said. 'Good!'

'Donald, I want to lay the table,' Sophie said.

'Right. Good!' The dentist sprang to attention. More rustling of pages.

Eliot didn't think about the book until after supper. Noni, tearing round the house in her usual frantic gathering of homework, was calling, 'Where's my Wilfred Owen?' Eliot ran into the hall and felt in his anorak pocket. Dismayed, he remembered how he had run from the riverbank, leaving the book on the damp bench.

'I'm sorry,' he began. 'It was in my pocket and I . . .'

'In your pocket? How come?' Noni stood on the bottom stair, hands accusingly on hips.

'Someone put it there by accident, I guess,' Eliot's explanation was already in tatters, 'so I went with it, or rather it went with me . . .' he rambled on.

'Where is it now? That's all I want to know.'

'Not here,' said Eliot lamely.

'Then where?' demanded Noni.

'Please,' Donald's head appeared round the sitting-room door. 'Would it be possible for you to speak a little quieter? I'm trying to listen to the news.'

'Eliot's lost my book,' barked Noni.

'Ah.' The dentist disappeared.

'I haven't lost your book,' Eliot said. 'I left it on the bench. It's still in the park I guess.' He could feel himself getting panicky.

'You guess! You guess! Your whole life's just a guessing game, isn't it, Eliot Latimer?'

'Noni, don't be so mean,' Violet called from the top of the stairs.

Noni swore at her sister, who quickly withdrew her head. There was a touch of fury about Noni that kept surprising Eliot. Small kindnesses were often followed by sudden savage taunts. Once he could have coped but now he shied away from them. 'I'll go get it, right now,' he said. 'It must be there. No one's gonna steal an old poetry book.'

'I'll come with you,' Noni offered. She grinned. 'Sorry, but I'll get detention if I don't get something down about those damn poems by tomorrow.'

'They're good,' said Eliot quietly. He opened the front door and stared at the step in disbelief.

'What is it?' Noni saw what had so astonished Eliot. 'There. You dropped it.'

'No,' Eliot shook his head.

'Then someone followed you, and left it here.' Noni picked up the little book.

'No one followed me, except . . .' The world round Eliot began to sway, his legs felt weak and he wanted to be sick. He clung to the door frame, remembering the tap of invisible feet, the unseen hand rapping on the black door, the enveloping scent of flowers.

Noni drew him into the house and closed the door. 'You OK?'

'I guess,' he murmured. 'What else can I say? Maybe my life *is* a guessing game. I can *guess*, but I don't *know*.'

'Say you think you're OK!' said Noni amiably. 'But you're not sure!'

'I'm not sure,' he repeated miserably. He was sure of one thing, however. He was being haunted.

4

Sweet rocket

'Perhaps it was that woman,' Violet suggested when Eliot told her about the book. 'Freya Greymark.'

They were alone in the kitchen, Noni having retreated to her room with the Wilfred Owen. It was easier talking to Violet. She took everything so calmly. Her mellow grey eyes rested on him kindly and with interest. She seemed older than Noni, never a year younger.

'Why should it be Freya Greymark?' he asked.

'She seemed to have a strange effect on you, and she's peculiar, even Mum says so. She could have followed you without your knowing.'

'It wasn't her.' He thought of the woman's ring, the melting softness of the pearl. 'It wasn't anyone.'

'Eliot, what are you trying to say?'

'I don't know what's happening, Vi. I felt sick to my stomach when I saw the book because I couldn't see what was out there, in the street. It was following me. I could smell it – that sounds crazy, but it was so strong. Like a whole field of flowers.'

'Plants always smell stronger after rain, especially in

the evening. The back gardens along here are full of sweet rocket.'

'Yeah? Then I guess she was carrying a whole bunch of the stuff.'

'Who?'

'I don't know.' He got up from the table and made for the door. 'Thanks, Violet.' Her gentle eyes grew puzzled and he longed for the comfort of explaining things to her, of describing the strange sensation of being followed by – by what? A ghost? Even Violet might not understand that.

Upstairs he could hear Noni reading aloud. She had a high, tuneful voice that did not at all suit the poems. Not those poems, anyway.

His door was slightly ajar and a thick scent issued from his room. Breathtaking. Fragrant. Eliot stood on the threshold, intrigued and apprehensive. Gingerly, he pushed the door further open. A strong slant of sunlight sliced through the room. It was filled with gleaming motes that swirled through the beam and across the small swing mirror on the chest of drawers. At first Eliot could sense nothing out of place and then his eyes were drawn to the mirror. Someone had traced a circle in the thin layer of dust on its surface; a circle broken at the base by a small oval. The mark was so faint, if he turned his head it almost disappeared. But who had made it?

Eliot walked across the landing and broke into Noni's sing-song renderings. 'Have you been in my room?'

She looked up, scowling. 'I'm trying to work.' He stood in the doorway, wondering at his sudden impulse.

After all, it was just a circle. 'Sorry, only . . . there's something there.'

'You look peculiar,' she said.

'Can you come? I want someone to see.' He wished she were Violet. He should have run downstairs, but Noni was closer.

'It'd better be good.' Noni followed him to his room.

'There,' he nodded at the mirror.

'I can't see anything.'

'A circle, drawn on the mirror!'

'So? Eliot, is this a joke?'

'No.' His voice sounded frail. 'Can't you see, Noni?'

'I can see that you haven't dusted your mirror. Is that why your hair's a mess?' She gave a quick laugh, trying to wipe the frown off his face.

'How about the flowers, then? Can you smell them?'

She sniffed the air. 'Your window's open.' Noni walked smartly across the room and shut the window. 'There!' When she moved through the sunbeam her hair took on a rich, tobacco colour.

'It's the ring.' His voice sounded distant even to himself. As soon as he uttered the word, the circle on the glass began to glimmer; the oval filled with a soft pearl-white and the surrounding gems, blue and ruby, dazzled him. He turned his face away, holding his head against the cool of the door frame.

Noni tried to lead him to a chair but he resisted, pulling away from the room. 'Let's go downstairs,' she suggested.

When she saw them, Violet said, anxiously, 'Mum's

gone out.' But then her practical nature took over and while Noni coaxed Eliot into a chair she made a cup of cocoa. Eliot sipped it slowly, like an invalid, aware that the sisters were exchanging glances. Until today he had tried not to show emotion of any kind, in case it overwhelmed him. But now he was scared and didn't care that the girls thought his mind was disturbed by grief. He let their sympathy enfold him. It felt so good. They made him believe that the awful image on the mirror hadn't existed and would be gone when he went back.

When Sophie came in and began to dish up the supper, Eliot felt so much better, she never guessed what had happened. The girls didn't tell her. They kept Eliot's trouble to themselves, something that only one of their generation could understand. They would tackle Eliot's grief together, without involving Sophie or the dentist. Eliot was surprised to find that he was pleased to see the sisters united, however temporarily. It made the house seem safer.

At bedtime Violet put a glass of milk beside his bed and Noni tucked a favourite bear of hers under his duvet. She asked if he'd like a book to borrow. Any book.

'The war poems,' he said. 'If you don't need them.'

'Eliot, do you think you should?' Noni glanced at her sister. 'It's depressing stuff.'

'You might not sleep,' said Violet.

'Please,' Eliot begged. 'It doesn't depress me. I'm – interested.'

Noni shrugged and fetched the book. Violet said, 'Call out if you need us. We don't mind.'

'I don't need *anyone*,' he tried not to sound irritated. 'I just felt strange for a bit. It's gone now.' He gave the thumbs up sign. 'I'm OK. Right?'

They peered at him from the door, calm Violet and earnest Noni. 'Night, Eliot,' they said in unison and closed his door.

Eliot glanced quickly at the mirror. One of the girls had wiped away the mysterious circle and polished the glass ferociously. Now his own reflection gleamed back at him. He opened the book and studied the portrait on the frontispiece. The poet as a soldier. He had a slight whimsical smile but the grave, dark-centred eyes seemed to Eliot like a warning. He found himself locked into the intense and tragic gaze, until everything in his room drifted out of focus. The poet's features blurred, and when Eliot attempted to draw them together, they settled into the planes of a quite different face. Abundant black hair framed a wide brow, the dark eyes grew rounder and the soldier's smile brought two long dimples to his cheeks.

Chill out, Eliot, he said to himself. He was trembling and contemplated going to watch late night television to take his mind off things. 'But I'm not grieving,' he said aloud, and switched off his light.

He woke up some time after midnight, feeling a drift of scented air across his face. The scent intensified until he thought that he would drown in it. Forced to sit up, he found himself looking at the mirror. And there it was. The ring. This time a true reflection, not an object sketched in dust. Now it hovered in the glass, as though

26

worn by an invisible finger. The rubies glistened like drops of blood.

Eliot flung back his head, screwing his eyes fast against the dark. He couldn't bring himself to call for help, he knew no one else would see what he could. He turned his back on the mirror, and spent the night falling in and out of sleep, eyelids pressed against the pillow and knees drawn tight into his chest.

When he appeared for breakfast, Sophie exclaimed, 'Darling, are you ill?'

He shook his head and took a place at the table. Noni and Violet, he saw, had already left for school.

'Just a few more weeks and the girls will be on holiday,' said Sophie. 'You'll have some daytime company then. They've planned all sorts of things.'

'Have they?' Eliot tried to sound enthusiastic.

'What would you like to do today?' Sophie folded plump arms on the table and smiled encouragingly. 'You've been so brave, Eliot. You have every right to . . . to let go now and again.' She stopped short of mentioning Lily. 'Shall we go somewhere, to take your mind off things?'

Eliot did not reply. His thoughts filled with the image of a ring. 'I'm being haunted,' he said.

Sophie frowned. 'Are you, darling? It's no wonder, really.'

'I don't think you understand,' said Eliot weakly. 'It's not . . . It's someone else. A sort of guardian angel. Or I thought so, once.'

'Oh!' She sat back, temporarily stumped.

'That woman,' Eliot went on. 'Freya Greymark. I keep seeing her ring – in my mind.'

'Mm.' Sophie forced a smile. 'I see.'

'Why d'you think that is?'

'Well, Eliot,' Sophie paused. 'I think it's just a symptom of your . . . loss.'

It didn't sound logical to him. Why *that* ring? It wasn't Lily's style at all. His mother wore silver. She loved large semi-precious stones: moss agate, opals and topaz. Silver bangles chimed on her pale arms, silver hoops glinted between tendrils of her thick, blonde hair.

'And then there are the flowers,' he quickly averted his glistening eyes from Sophie's face. 'The smell follows me, and sometimes it's in my room. You'll say that's easy to explain because of the gardens out back, but it's not like that.'

Sophie stood up, holding out her hand. 'Come outside with me, Eliot.'

He took the hand and allowed himself to be led through the house and down into the walled garden at the back. Bright spring poppies grew there, mauve and white cranesbill, pink geraniums and yellow daisies. And beneath a rose-tree, not yet in bloom, there was a cluster of tall stems, each one frosted with a scattering of small starry flowers, some palest pink, others a deeper shade, almost purple.

'Sweet rocket,' Sophie told him, pointing to the starlike flowers. 'It has a wonderful scent, or it could be some other flower that you can smell.'

'No.' Eliot bent over the sweet rocket. 'It's this. Has

it always been here?'

'Probably. It's very prolific. The seed scatters and springs up everywhere, even between paving stones. In the evening its scent is very potent.

'But I smell it at night, with the windows closed.'

'I'm sure there's a simple explanation,' she said cheerfully. 'I've got to pop out to the post now, Eliot. But I'll wait till you've had your breakfast if you want to come for the walk, and then we'll go somewhere if you like.'

'No thanks. I'm OK.' He followed her indoors.

'By the way,' she said. 'Noni took a book out of your room while you were sleeping. But Violet found another she thought you might like. It's on the dresser in the sitting-room.'

Eliot found the small, squarish book. It was bound in deep red vellum with marbled endpapers. The tooling was gold. *'Orlando Furioso,'* Eliot read. 'Retold by V. Arditti.' He thumbed through it. Why had Violet chosen it for him? It was old and lavishly illustrated. There were flying horses, witches, castles and crusaders, and even a knight on the moon. The hero appeared to be one Orlando, a knight of the Emperor Charlemagne. It was the kind of book his mother would have chosen.

He was carrying the book into the kitchen when the doorbell rang. Eliot stopped and stood very still. Once, he had enjoyed talking to strangers, but now he was tempted to ignore the bell, pretend the house was empty.

The chimes rang out again, continuously, as though someone had fallen on the bell-push. Somehow Eliot did not think it could be Freya Greymark. Hers were sharp, brief summonses. He put the book on the hall table and reluctantly opened the door. 'I'm afraid everyone's out . . .' he began, but the old man on the step wasn't interested in anything Eliot had to say.

'Got a chair, lad?' he mumbled, pushing past Eliot. 'Where's the waiting-room?'

'There isn't one.'

The old man wasn't listening. 'Ah, here we are!' He bustled into the Pipers' sitting-room. 'No patients, then? Thank the Lord. Gum's on fire. How long to wait?'

'Could be hours,' said Eliot, pulling himself together.

'No cheek, boy. I'm an emergency.' The stranger's jaw was definitely swollen. He kept pressing a damp-looking handkerchief to his mouth.

'Gee, I'm sorry, but the dentist doesn't work here. His surgery's four blocks away, about that anyway, and he could be booked up all morning.'

'Blocks,' mumbled the old man. 'What blocks?'

'Blocks of houses,' Eliot said testily. 'Streets, I guess.'

'Huh! You're not from round here.'

'No. I've been in America.'

'I can tell. You talk different, don't you?' The man himself had a thick rural accent, rolling his r's and lengthening his vowels considerably. But Eliot didn't feel like arguing.

'What's to be done then, boy. This used to be the dentist's. My old tooth needs attention, *now*.'

'Come with me.' Eliot had cautiously allowed a memory into his head.

In the kitchen, he put a teaspoon of salt in a mug and poured boiling water on to it. He topped this up with cold water from the tap and handed it to the patient. 'Just swill it round the sore place and spit it out,' he said.

'You a dentist, or what?' The patient looked suspicious.

'It's something my mother did for me once. It worked. My name's Eliot, by the way.'

'Fred Bean.' The old man shook Eliot's free hand and grasped the mug with the other. He took his medicine seriously, salt water swirled in his cheek like dish water in a drain, and then he retched, rather than spat, into the sink. After several minutes, he slammed the empty mug on the draining-board and sat back at the table. 'It's working,' he declared. 'Clever lad.'

'My mother's remedies always work,' Eliot said softly.

'She a dentist too, then?'

'No, I'm kinda visiting with the Pipers. Mr Piper, he's the dentist.'

Fred Bean wiped the stubble on his chin. 'Used to live here,' he said.

'You? In this house?' Eliot was astonished.

'No, no. Salter Row. Number six.'

'Next to number seven?' Eliot thought of the black door, the bronze hawk.

'Opposite. I were a four year old. Never forget some things.'

'Like what?' asked Eliot eagerly.

'Bread queues. Feeling hungry. Dad joining up, ever so proud of his new uniform. The Great War. Tst!' Eliot had the impression that the old man would have spat on the floor, had he not been in a stranger's kitchen.

'Can you remember anything – out of the ordinary?'

'Everything were out of the ordinary. Out of this world. My dad never came back. Ma was tore up with grief. Couldn't afford the house in Salter Row no more, so back we goes to my grandad's farm. Happened a lot then. Funny how we remember things like that, when yesterday's business is forgotten in a blink.'

Eliot had been watching the old man hungrily. 'Can you . . .?' he asked tentatively. 'Can you remember anything special about number seven Salter Row?'

'Course I can.' Fred Bean coughed then cleared his throat. 'Never forget it. The girl standing there. We still had gas lamps in our street then. Different sort of light. Eerie!'

'And the girl?' breathed Eliot.

'Dark. Only a slip of a thing. Seventeen, eighteen maybe. She'd lost her sweetheart, you see. Never came back from the war, like my own poor dad. But that girl was took worse than my ma. Mad, she was. Gone. Wailing like a banshee.'

'Just wails?' asked Eliot. 'No words?' He could almost hear her voice. Her face, pale as the moon, shone with tears.

'Mm!' Fred sucked his teeth. 'Maybe.'

'Oh!' said Sophie's voice. 'Who?' She strode into the room. 'What's going on?'

'A patient has come here . . .' stammered Eliot trying to hold tight to his vision.

'Fred Bean!' Fred stood up, took Sophie's hand and

shook it warmly. 'Came to see the dentist. Your lad here fixed me up a treat.'

'But the surgery is . . .' Sophie nodded at the door, frowning, 'a mile away. If you want to make a proper appointment . . .'

'Reckon I'd better.'

Sophie ushered Fred Bean out of the kitchen, rather hurriedly, Eliot thought. He followed them, desperate to put more questions.

'Come and see us, lad,' Fred called back. 'Dove Farm. We don't farm any more, bones too far gone for that, but Mrs Bean likes company. And you ought to see a bit of real country before you go home. It's half a mile out of Hallowater.'

'Home?' Sophie looked at Eliot.

'To America,' Eliot said, turning from Sophie's anxious frown. 'I'll come, Mr Bean. I'll borrow a bike.'

Sophie opened the door and the old man stepped out. 'The surgery's just off the main road,' she said. 'Vincent Street. You can't miss it. Number three. I'm sorry you've had all this trouble. But Mr Piper hasn't had a surgery here for . . . oh, years. Five, I should say.'

'Ah, five years since I've needed him,' Fred grunted. Then he turned suddenly and said to Eliot, 'About that girl, Flowers it was.'

'What sort of flowers?' asked Eliot, thinking of the crushing scent in his bedroom.

'No, no.' Fred shook his head. 'Not *flowers*. It was her name. Mary-Ellen Flowers. I saw her again, but not here, oh no. It was out at the farm. Fancy me remembering that,' and he walked away quite briskly for an old man whose bones were too far gone.

'I *will* come,' Eliot called after him. 'On Saturday.'

'Eliot, you mustn't let people in like that.' Sophie closed the door firmly.

'I didn't have a choice,' Eliot told her. 'Honest. He just came at me, holding his jaw. It seemed kinda mean not to help. But it was like fate, wasn't it? He told me some stuff about the time he lived here. In the Great War. Stuff about the girl . . .' He hardly understood where all this was leading him. 'Sophie, I can go to Dove Farm, can't I?'

'I've no idea where it is.'

'We'll find it. Maybe Noni or Violet can come with me. And I'll borrow one of their bikes.'

'You'll be lucky,' Sophie said, 'the state their bikes are in.'

'I'm serious, Sophie.'

'Of course you can,' she said gently. 'We'll look it up on the map.'

That afternoon, Eliot went round to Salter Row again. He stood opposite number seven and tried to imagine the house as it had been, nearly eighty years ago. He'd been there less than a minute when he heard the sobbing. It echoed across to him, heavy with pain, crushing Eliot with its grief until he found himself sinking under the burden of sound. And yet there was no one there. He covered his ears with his hands but the tears and grief were in his head and he couldn't banish them.

The door of number seven opened and a woman stood there; tall and darkly dressed, her hair piled on her head in steely swathes, her eyes the savage yellow of an eagle. 'Go away,' she said to Eliot.

'Where's the ring?' he asked.

At that, she swooped across the road and, clawing at Eliot's shoulder, rasped, 'You ought to be locked up!'

He tried to shrug her off, twisting and turning beneath her hand, while she sighed and groaned as though wrestling with some terrible demon of her own. At last he broke free and, looking up, saw that it was Freya Greymark. His shoulder ached from the grip of her sinewy fingers.

'Who are you, boy?' she said. 'Why are you spying on me?'

Eliot rubbed his head and murmured, 'What did you do to her?'

'What are you talking about?' said Freya. 'What do you want?'

'Where's the ring?' he whispered, gazing at her bare right hand.

She thrust her hand behind her back. 'American!' she hissed. 'Go home!'

He had to pull himself up by the railings of number six, he felt so dizzy. Behind him he could see a boy's puzzled face at the window. Must think I'm a nut, thought Eliot. 'Don't feel so good,' he said to the woman.

She turned on her heel and hurried over to her own door, closing it fast behind her, sliding the bolt. The brass hawk glittered against black paint.

Eliot grinned sheepishly at the puzzled boy and walked back to Fly Street. He felt exhausted and went straight to his room to gather his wits. All he wanted was peace and a space in his mind to think.

But someone had been there. Violent hands had pulled, torn, flung and smashed. Bedclothes, boxes, clothes and books lay in chaos. And the mirror had a crack like a sunburst, exactly where the ring had glistened.

5
Break-in

He stood inside the door, trying to believe he was dreaming; hoping that, somehow, the past had imposed itself on this small room. He had been tipped back into history, very briefly, and if he closed his eyes the world would right itself. Books, clothes and bedding would fly back into place, and in a moment the bed would be smooth and tidy with its matching covers, a safe and comfortable place to sleep.

But the chaos didn't go. And, all at once, Eliot was angry. Someone real had made this mess. He stormed downstairs to find Sophie.

She was in the room that had once been the surgery. A bright room with pale, steel-legged furniture, dominated by her computer. She was sitting at her desk while a printer buzzed beside her.

'Sophie, someone's been in my room,' he said.

'Not while you were out.' She didn't take her eyes from the machine.

'Yes, they have,' he insisted. 'There's a horrible mess.'

This time she looked at him. She pushed her blue-framed spectacles up the bridge of her nose and said, 'Perhaps I'd better see.'

'Yeah!' He led the way, leaping up the stairs, two at a time.

Sophie, a bit puffed from rising two floors at a faster pace than she was used to, followed him into his room. 'Eliot!' she exclaimed. Her eyes rested on the cracked mirror. 'What happened?'

'You tell me,' he said. 'Someone came in here.'

'I've been in my study since you left. I'd have seen. No one's been in the house.'

'Then who did this?' he demanded, his voice cracking with the effort of trying to disguise his alarm.

'I don't know, darling. Let's tidy up.' She moved through the room, straightening covers, folding his clothes, patting books into shelves and cupboards.

Eliot, watching and trying to help, asked, 'Are you going to ring the police?'

'I don't think so,' Sophie said quietly and without looking at him.

'But something's happened here.'

'Yes.' She straightened up and regarded Eliot with a calm smile. 'I don't want you to worry about it.'

'You bet I'm worried. Someone broke in.' He glanced at the sash window and noticed the bars outside. They ran, like the rungs of a ladder, the whole length of the window frame. Even though the window could be opened, nothing larger than a head could be thrust through the bars. No one had entered that way. 'Why is the window barred?' he asked.

'I've no idea. Perhaps to stop a little child from falling

out. They've always been here, the bars, since we came.'

Eliot had not noticed, at first, how intense was the scent of flowers. When he did he said dully, 'It's her.'

'What are you talking about, Eliot?' Sophie couldn't hide her impatience. 'D'you mean that woman, Mrs Greymark?'

'No. She was solid. She couldn't swim through plaster or fly through glass, carry armfuls of invisible flowers.'

'Then who, Eliot?'

'The person who is . . .' he couldn't use the word 'haunting'. It was continually misinterpreted. Avoiding Sophie's concerned scrutiny he said, 'It was just a "happening".' And he grinned self-consciously.

With an arm round his shoulder, Sophie marched Eliot downstairs. 'I wish the girls were on holiday,' she said. 'You should be getting out more, doing things. How about going for a drive this evening? It's light until nine o'clock. We could go out to Benford. There's more to do there. Noni loves indoor bowling, and she won't have homework tonight.'

How she could chatter. Eliot smiled and murmured, 'OK' to everything that Sophie said. But his thoughts were with the guardian angel. Why had she become so violent?

He spent the afternoon batting a ball against the garden wall. He sang under his breath, trying to compose a rhythm to match his strokes. An hour must have slipped by without his noticing because when he was coming back through the French windows in the sitting-room, he could hear voices in the kitchen. The girls were home. For some reason, Eliot moved as quietly as he could. The voices were pitched low. An urgent discussion was taking place, and he knew he was the subject.

'He must know he did it. So why pretend?' This was Noni's voice.

Sophie said, 'I honestly don't think he knew. He looked so frightened.'

'I'd have been frightened,' Violet's voice could only just be heard.

Eliot crept soundlessly upstairs. He felt like a jelly. The whole of his inside seemed to be shaking. They believed he was making it up. They thought that it was he who had made the havoc in his room, and that he didn't know it.

He sat on the bed, shivering. 'It's your fault,' he said, not too loud. 'But why me? Can't you haunt someone else?'

A sigh stole through the perfumed air. The cracked mirror glittered threateningly and a fragment of glass fell on to the dressing-table. It made a sound like a tiny bell. Eliot approached the mirror. The splinter of broken glass was slim and fatally sharp. He picked it up and slipped it into the drawer in his bedside table. 'There,' he found himself saying to his unseen companion, 'now you know where to find it.' A cool breath fluttered across his face.

'I'm tired,' he said wearily. 'Give me some space now, will you?'

He sensed the emptiness she left behind, as she breezed away. Where to? he wondered.

Steering clear of the events in Eliot's room, the

conversation at suppertime was carried on in a tone of uneasy cheerfulness. Eliot sat glum and silent while Violet and Noni chattered affectionately and Sophie interposed with bright comments. Only the dentist, unaware of what had happened, acted with his usual quiet composure.

Noni began to badger Eliot with questions about his father; where he worked, how long he stayed abroad. Eliot answered with shrugs and monosyllables, he didn't want to talk about his father. At last he said, 'Will someone come to Hallowater with me?'

'Why?' asked Noni, surprised but glad to have got a sentence out of him.

'I just want to go there. Someone invited me.'

'Who?' begged Violet and Noni, intrigued that Eliot had made a friend.

'An old man,' he told them, and in spite of their obvious disappointment, went on to describe Fred Bean and his memories of life in Salter Row. 'The wailing girl was called Mary-Ellen Flowers,' he said.

The dentist looked up. 'She lived here,' he said with a pleased expression.

'Here?' said Noni, instantly intrigued.

'Here?' Eliot's fingers knotted together in his lap.

'Mm,' murmured the dentist. 'My father bought the house from a Mr Flowers in '48. Daughter long gone by then. Sad. Very sad. I believe they had to lock her up.'

His tone was casual but the words burned into Eliot's head and grew there into a picture of startling clarity: a room of mahogany darkness, lofty, polished cupboards, black-framed watercolours of the town, a white tablecloth bedecked with glinting silver, and a tall man wrapped tight in a black coat. Gaslight threw his brooding shadow towards Eliot, and the monotonous beat of a clock hung behind the sound of tears. But who was crying?

Gradually the real everyday faces of Violet and Noni swam through to him. Sharp voices pierced the sobbing. 'Eliot, what is it?' 'Eliot, where are you? Can you hear us?'

'Sorry,' he muttered as the gloomy room receded. 'Something kind of strange just happened.'

'I'll come to Hallowater with you,' Noni's voice made itself heard above the others.

Eliot tried to show that he was pleased, but found that he couldn't. He was overcome by someone else's grief, and could only say, 'I'll never smile again.' But it wasn't what he meant, it wasn't even his voice.

'Oh, Eliot, darling, of course you will,' cried Sophie, coming quickly to his side. 'I don't mind about the room.' Her arm was round his shoulder, his cheek pressed into the soft ribs of a corduroy jacket.

'We'll both come to Hallowater with you,' said Violet. 'Tonight I'm going to mend all the punctures. And we can hire a bike for Eliot, can't we, Dad?'

'Might as well buy one,' said the dentist. 'Got to have a bike, I imagine. Good idea!' he congratulated himself.

'Brilliant,' cheered Noni. 'We'll choose one after school tomorrow, shall we?'

'It's Eliot's bike,' Sophie reminded her.

'I'd like some company,' he said.

That night Sophie took the broken mirror out of Eliot's room. She didn't put anything in its place. He told her he would use the bathroom mirror to brush his hair. 'I guess I don't need one at all,' he said.

The room seemed smaller, somehow. The walls loomed in at him, patterned with tiny flowers, drenched in perfume. And all at once it came to him. Mary-Ellen slept here, in this room. Or lay awake, recalling some precious time when a soldier stood outside the house, calling her name. Would she have looked through the bars? Why were they there? 'They had to lock her up,' the dentist had said. Was this room her prison, then?

Eliot swung his feet out of bed and went to the window. The street outside was deserted. It must have been well after midnight. A few cars rolled down the High Street. The night was muggy and starless. A sound began in the distance and swelled until it seemed to be entering Fly Street: a crunching, rhythmic drumming. It billowed closer, not thunder or machinery of any sort; it had an unresisting dreadful doggedness, and as it crescendoed towards Eliot he recognised the beat of marching feet. As they passed the house, he saw them: a regiment of ghostly volunteers in dull khaki. He saw their glinting regimental badges, their backs braided with canvas straps, leather holsters and bayonets. One man looked up at Eliot and gave a bleak smile. His eyes were hidden by his peaked hat.

And then they were gone. Only the sound remained, a tide of boots receding like water, until the march was a faraway trickle that eventually died.

A cold shudder began deep inside Eliot, and raced through his veins like a circuit of ice. 'So,' he kept repeating. 'So. Now I get it.' And he resigned himself to the fact that Mary-Ellen had chosen to impose her tragedy on him. Perhaps sharing made it easier for her. But he wished that she had chosen someone else. Will I have to relive all of it? he wondered. He was so tired he could barely drag his legs beneath the bedclothes.

He slept very late next morning. When he woke up the room was filled with an unfamiliar brightness. He had left the curtains open and the sun was shining in on him.

Sophie poked her head round the door. 'We let you sleep,' she said. 'Want a cooked breakfast?'

'It's eleven o'clock.' Eliot grabbed at his watch. 'I'm sorry.'

'Bacon and eggs?' Sophie smiled. 'Waffles and honey?'

'You don't have to spoil me.'

'I'm hungry myself. I was up at six. Wanted to do some baking before I got down to work. I don't like eating alone.'

'OK. Waffles and honey.' Eliot felt lighter, somehow. The sunshine helped. Perhaps he would have some peace, today.

After breakfast he strolled down to the river. A group of downy bundles skimmed across the water behind a swan. The cygnets were on display. Walking close to the sparkling water, Eliot began to follow them. But when he reached a bench he sat down and took out the book he had brought. The name on the flyleaf didn't surprise him.

M-E Flowers. The letters were small and neatly formed. Hardly remarkable, except, of course, they were *hers*. She had touched the book, carried it in a pocket, breathed on the yellowing pages, pushed it under her pillow. He didn't have to bring it close to his face to smell the flowers. The paper reeked of it. He sat with the book in his hands, letting her reach him. He could sense another bout of violence approaching and wanted her to have a few moments of peace, watching the cygnets on the tranquil water through his eyes.

When he went back he avoided Salter Row and the door with the shiny brass hawk, but he couldn't avoid Fly Street and that's where he heard the cry. But before the cry there came another sound, the creak of a wheel right beside him, and the clop-clop of a cart horse that wasn't there, and in the air he saw a cloud of falling flowers.

July 1917

Mary-Ellen comes down Fly Street. She has just taken a pie to Lizzie Dove. Poor woman, she's not yet thirty and has seven mouths to feed. Bertie Dove was killed in action, just two months ago. Nancy, her eldest, is only twelve but almost as tall as Mary-Ellen. So along with the pie, Mary-Ellen took a bundle of clothes she didn't need and a book she'd been fond of when she was twelve. Louisa May Alcott's *Little Women*.

And Nancy had to rush out into their small back

garden, where sweet rocket spindled up above the weeds. A tall, starlike, vigorous flower with a scent that Nancy says is like heaven. The girl snipped at the stems with her sewing scissors until her arms were full of flowers, and she thrust them at Mary-Ellen saying, tearfully, 'You're so good to us. We can't ever properly thank you. I hope and pray your young man comes home, like our poor dad never will.'

Now Mary-Ellen is swamped in flowers. The sky is so blue today and the air has a special crystal clarity. It must be a good omen. Orlando *will* come home.

A rag-and-bone cart rumbles over the cobbles behind her. And she remembers the leaflet from the Ministry of Food. They must save grease from the washing-up water and sell it to the rag-and-bone man. The fat thus collected will provide glycerine for ammunition – already the army kitchens have saved enough to make propellant for 18,000,000 shells.

All at once, Mary-Ellen stands very still, under the sun, wondering if, over in Germany, they are skimming their sinks and giving the grease to the rag-and-bone men. Wondering who is responsible for the shell that killed Bertie Dove. Lloyd George? The King? Or a German housewife just doing her duty? Mary-Ellen's heartbeat quickens, though she has not exerted herself. Her steps are not so fast now. She walks up the slight incline towards the house and sees them, her mother in the doorway and Mr Rinaldi in his black suit and bowler, standing on the step.

Mr Rinaldi turns a gaunt face to Mary-Ellen, and

Mrs Flowers' hand has flown to her lips.

A scream breaks out of Mary-Ellen. 'No! No! No!' Her body is tearing apart. She flings out her arms, trying to breathe and sprays of sweet rocket fly into the street, straight into the path of the rag-and-bone man. The blinkered cart-horse hardly notices, his great iron shoes trample the flowers and the air is filled with their fragrance. On Mary-Ellen's skin it will be indelible.

6
The drowning

The bike Eliot chose was black. He stood under the
pitiless store lights surrounded by gleaming metal, and it
seemed to be the only one that matched his thoughts.

The ghostly sounds had lasted only a few seconds; a
moment snatched from the past and trapped in his head
so swiftly that Eliot barely had time to draw breath. And
yet, here they were again, and here were the falling
flowers vivid and more real than the banks of glossy
machines. And in Eliot's ear the creak of a wheel and the
metallic clip of hooves on stone, cutting through the
busy chatter that surrounded him.

'I shall call you Elly, if you keep going funny like that!'
Noni said, peering into his face.

So Eliot banished the sounds and made a face he
thought was suitable, a big smile of pleasure. 'Thanks!'

'Don't thank me, Eliot!' The dentist was grinning like
a schoolboy. He had enjoyed browsing round the store of
mountain bikes, half-pretending he was choosing a bike
for himself.

'Gilbert said you must have one. Your dad was in on
this, Eliot.' Sophie squeezed his arm. 'He'll be back in

London tonight. D'you want to phone him?'

'Sure!' He took the handlebars and began to wheel the bike out.

They wouldn't let him ride home. 'You've got to get the hang of keeping to the left,' Sophie told him. 'A trip to Dove Farm will help.' And he wondered if the family had made a pact to guard and watch him. At the moment, Noni was more interested in the bicycle.

'No mudguard,' she observed. 'You'll get sloshed all up the back.'

'Who cares?' said Eliot cheerfully.

'You wait,' said Noni. 'Hallowater's all cows, I bet!'

That night he telephoned his father, but Gilbert was not at home; his voice on the answerphone was intimate and slightly rueful, it took Eliot through empty rooms where, once, his mother had moved, in bright colours, with silver glinting at her wrists and her hair a sort of halo. It seemed pointless to leave a message. He replaced the receiver without giving his name.

In the early hours next morning, a fierce north-easterly blew up, it drove torrents of icy rain into the streets, and howled round the roofs of Saintbury. But Eliot slept peacefully. Even the scent of flowers had faded from his room. Mary-Ellen was allowing him to gather his strength. Perhaps, soon, he would be able to guess what she wanted of him.

On Saturday he woke at six, and had finished breakfast long before the girls were up. When they finally appeared, Eliot sat and watched their sleepy movements until Noni grumbled, 'Stop it, Elly! You're giving me indigestion!'

'Rose Red!' he countered. 'She was the bad-tempered one!'

Violet gazed anxiously over the rim of her teacup and shook her head. 'Not bad-tempered,' she said, 'impatient.'

Her attempt to pacify Noni didn't work.

'Snow White. White as snow. Angel white!' growled Noni. But whatever storm was brewing in Noni had blown over by the time they wheeled their bikes out into the road.

Sophie watched anxiously. 'Single file,' she said. 'Eliot between you two girls.'

But it was still early and the traffic was thin. As they sailed over the bridge the sun came out. They turned off the main road and almost immediately were surrounded by fields of brilliant green.

Noni sang as she rode through the ocean of grasses. Her strong voice threw the tune at the sky, and Violet began to accompany her. Crows lifted from the fields and swung, cawing over their heads. And Eliot, encircled by exuberant voices, warm air and swaying shades of green, felt as though he were flying.

The fields were bisected by a myriad of narrow lanes, marked by signposts where they crossed each other. In many cases the signs had turned in the wind, letters had faded and wood cracked. At each post Noni would dismount and study the names: Hodstone, Slipperfoot, Sallowfield, Hokum, Spillover, Wim, Harefrost, Grassing. She would stand with her hands clasped behind her back, repeat the names and then swing round to face them. 'We're getting there,' she would announce.

Once Violet called, 'Have you ever seen anything like this, Eliot? It could be the sea.'

And although Eliot squeezed his mind tight, he was not fast enough to stop the quick stab of memory: Gilbert's hands on the steering-wheel and Lily fast asleep beside him. Through the window, fields rushing by, mile after mile, but gold not green. Eliot's small fingers creeping forward to wake his mother. Gilbert's voice, 'Don't wake her!' And Lily with her eyes closed, smiling.

'This is nothing,' Eliot dismissed the rolling fields. 'Ever heard of the corn belt?'

'Silly me!' said Violet.

They stopped for a snack in a café in Hodstone, and when they came out the breeze had sharpened and turned into their faces. They lowered their heads and bulldozed into it. Noni whizzed past a sign whose letters made no sense at all, and Violet called, 'D'you really know where you're going, Noni?'

'I know,' sang Noni. 'I'm excellent with maps. We're nearly there. Watch out. Here we go!'

All at once they were descending into a hidden valley. The lane became a narrow street with red-brick cottages on either side, neat Victorian buildings still roofed in slate. Most had a fenced front garden and neighbours had clearly been competing. Flowers crowded round paths, billowed over fences and curled under windows. Every gate was numbered, there were no names. So Violet stopped a woman turning under a swinging post office sign, and asked, 'Is there a farm near here. Dove Farm?'

'Half a mile out, dear.' The woman had a rich country accent. 'Can't miss it. It's on the road. You want Beans or Dilhursts?'

'Beans,' said Eliot.

'Too old to work the farm, poor dears. No kids. It's up to the Dilhursts now. The Beans live in the farmhouse though. Not big enough for the Dilhursts. Not by a long chalk. Not grand enough. They had to have something better, didn't they?'

The Dilhursts obviously were not popular in some quarters. Violet thanked the woman and the three cyclists rode out of the hamlet. The road became a lane again, with such a steep incline they were forced to dismount and push the bikes. A shadowy track branched off to their left. Half-hidden in a tangle of weeds, Eliot saw a peeling sign. He stopped, and words fell almost soundlessly from his lips. 'This way.'

Violet caught up and began to pass him. 'What is it, Eliot?'

Eliot nodded at the sign. His throat felt dry and he tried to swallow. A terrible pressure inside his head muffled sound and blurred leaves and flowers into a swaying sea.

Violet spied the sign. '*D v arm*. Not much left. This way, Noni!'

Noni turned her bike and the girls raced up the track. The land levelled and they leaped on their saddles and began to pedal. 'Come on, Eliot,' Noni called. 'I can see the farmhouse.'

On either side, tall hedges loomed, starry with flowers. Hawthorn and elderflower: a sharp, sweet tang from long ago. And, once again, Eliot was not alone. He sensed her small, leather-clad feet stepping beside him and something else, a companion. Their silent laughter drifted about the lane like sprays of sunlight. And Eliot knew what he would find when he turned the corner: a cobbled farmyard with stables on either side; a wagon of hay, its contents spilling on to the cobbles; a huge shire horse drinking from a trough; red chickens everywhere, one with a family of chicks; and the slates of the stable, white with sleeping doves.

It was not quite like that, but so similar that Eliot had to stop and take a breath before he went through the gate.

'Come on, Eliot. This is your visit!' Violet called.

The girls were already crossing the yard to a neat brick porch. The house itself was hidden behind a curtain of ivy. There was only a hint of stone here and there, to show that a solid wall existed behind the leaves. Four windows peeped through the greenery, two above and two below, like the portholes of a sinking ship . . .

The stables were empty, the yard deserted. But the stone trough was there, and on one of the stable roofs, a flock of doves dozed in the sun. As Eliot paused to look at them, the wind lifted the birds and tossed them in a murmuring cloud above his head. They fanned over the house and were swallowed by the brilliant sky.

A very small person had opened the porch door, and now stood talking to Violet and Noni. Noni beckoned

Eliot and, balancing his bike beside the others against a wall, he moved closer to the group.

'We didn't expect three,' the woman was saying. 'Fred just said a boy.'

'We had to bring him. He didn't know the way,' Noni explained. 'Are we too many?'

'Good gracious, no. The more the merrier.' The little woman had a face like a round, brown nut, and her curly hair still had streaks of russet in it. Eliot marvelled that she had expected anyone at all. The invitation had been rather casual.

They were ushered down a narrow passage and into the kitchen. Fred Bean sat at the end of a long kitchen table; a table spread for visitors, with cold meat and potato salad, bread and butter, biscuits and several sorts of cake.

'There you are, lad!' Fred beamed at Eliot.

'Hi, Mr Bean!' Eliot was astonished by the spread.

Mrs Bean insisted they wash their hands in the giant sink, like small children coming in from play. When they sat down they found they were hungry enough to all but finish the unexpected feast. While they ate, Mrs Bean told them about the farm that had belonged to Fred's grandfather. How it had thrived, small but efficient because of the rich land. She told them of the lost boys, Fred's father and three uncles who, like her own father, hadn't survived the Great War. 'Not one came back to Hallowater,' she said with a sigh.

'Not one,' echoed the old man.

The silence in the yard outside seemed to Eliot like

another silence. The void left by the missing. And he felt a small flicker of rage that wasn't entirely his own.

'Sixteen lads left here before 1918, I'm told!' said Mrs Bean. 'Proud as kings, but meek as lambs really. I were only a three year old, so I don't remember too much about them times. But talk, talk, talk, my auntie used to go on so much it's like I saw it all with my own eyes. The war swallowed them up one by one, until there were no more left.'

'D'you mean that no one who left to fight ever came back?' asked Violet.

Mrs Bean shook her head. 'Not from here. But that weren't the worst of it. It were the girls they left. No children to look for, ever. No men. No hope of a home, unless they stayed with their folks. They, like, faded. You'd see them years after, and you'd know they'd lost someone. One or two couldn't accept it, they went wild, especially when they heard the truth.'

'The truth?' said Eliot.

'That those poor boys died for nothing,' growled Fred. 'Sent over the top, straight into the guns, not an inch of ground gained. Cannon fodder they called them. Food for guns, all because of a few folks at the top. Ministers, generals and such like thought that human beings were nothing when it came to winning.'

No one knew how to follow this outburst. Fred still seemed to be fighting for the lost souls of the Great War, even though other wars and other soldiers had been lost. And then Fred suddenly turned to Eliot and said, almost fiercely, 'You're here for Mary-Ellen, aren't you, lad?'

Her name, spoken like that, shocked Eliot. It was like something secret unexpectedly thrust into the light. 'Yes,' he said, and he was aware of the girls' faces, blank because he couldn't bring himself to look at them, and yet, somehow burning with interest.

'How d'you mean, "for her"?' Noni asked.

'He knows what I mean,' Fred nodded at Eliot.

'It's happened before, you see,' Mrs Bean spoke in a soothing voice. 'When Fred told me a boy had been asking about number seven, I knew somehow it was on account of Mary-Ellen. Don't ask me how. I knew. It just seemed well . . .'

'It happened before?' exclaimed Eliot. 'D'you mean someone saw the . . . did she haunt them?' He glanced at the girls' stunned faces.

'In a way. That's why we knew when it happened again. Only the second time . . . Oh my, it were much, much worse.'

Nothing could have proclaimed their interest more than the awed silence that followed. Mrs Bean continued, cautiously at first, because she had to feel her way back into the strange events that had taken place so long ago. 'With Tom, our Nancy's boy, it were only a hint. Nancy is Fred's cousin by the way. Little Tom were five at the time, 1935 it was. He were running down Salter Row and Nancy were walking behind; she had the baby in a pram, but she kept her eye on Tom, naturally. Anyway, all of a sudden, Tom stops, right across from number seven, and his hand goes to his mouth, his eyes round as oranges. Nancy asks him, "What is it, Tom?"

And he says, "I can hear a lady crying something dreadful, but there's no one there," and he tucked his little hand in hers and it was like ice, Nancy said. And she could hardly bring herself to look across the road, but she did – and she saw her.'

'Mary-Ellen,' Fred said quietly.

'Our Nancy was very close to Mary-Ellen, loved her like a sister. So it's no wonder really.'

'But did she . . .' Eliot's throat was dry. 'Was Mary-Ellen there, or not?'

'Well, definitely not, of course,' said Mrs Bean, 'because she'd been dead and gone, fifteen years or more, hadn't she? On the other hand you could say that, for Nancy, she *were* there.'

'You mean a ghost, don't you?' Noni asked in her forthright way.

'Yes, dear, a ghost,' said Mrs Bean, unexpectedly matter-of-fact.

'And did she see her again, in different places?' inquired Noni.

'Never. That woman, Freya Greymark, the mother of the Freya that lives there now, she came out and said something to Mary-Ellen, and it was like she killed her all over again. That's what Nancy said.'

'Killed her?' In his mind's eye, Eliot saw the black door, the woman swooping out, and he felt the dreadful fingers on his shoulder.

'In a manner of speaking,' Fred told him, 'but that's only the way we see it. Mary-Ellen had a ring from her young man, you see.'

'A ring!' breathed Eliot.

'A pearl,' said Mrs Bean, 'with sapphires and rubies all round it. Very old. Precious. From the young man's family; they were Italian, you know. But a ruby fell out, I think it were a ruby, so Mary-Ellen gave it back to . . . to . . .'

'Orlando,' Fred supplied.

His wife beamed at him. 'Fred's memory's better than mine. She gave it to Orlando to have it fixed at the jeweller's.'

'Orlando,' muttered Noni. 'The name of a cat, Orlando.'

'An Italian name,' Fred told her.

'Orlando Furioso,' Eliot murmured, looking at Violet.

'I found a book,' said Violet, smiling round at everyone. 'It must have been hers; under the boards in the airing cupboard. No one would ever have found it, but I dropped my hockey pin down this crack, and I pulled at the board – and there it was. And I gave it to Eliot because it looked, kind of – well the sort of book he would like.'

'But the ring,' pressed Eliot. 'What happened to it?'

'Disappeared,' Fred said dramatically. 'Her young man went back to France with his regiment and never came back. He was killed in action and buried out there – far away. And when Mr Rinaldi,' he gave a jaunty nod at his wife, pleased at remembering the unusual name, 'when Mr Rinaldi went to collect the ring from the jeweller's, it had gone, been paid for and collected. They showed him the signed receipt, his own name, forged of course, but so well you couldn't tell the difference. We heard all this from the Rinaldis' neighbours. Mr Rinaldi died soon after, poor man; they said it was the flu. His wife was already gone, and then his favourite son.

'So Mary-Ellen never saw her ring again?' said Noni.

'Once,' said Mrs Bean, raising her eyebrows a fraction. 'Mrs Paget, who were on the ribbon counter at Rickman's, she told me about it years later. She told everyone. It were something she could never forget. Mrs Greymark, Miss Simnel as she were then, well, she were in the store asking to see some blue organdie, and she puts out her hand to feel the quality, and all at once someone grabs the hand so tight that Miss Simnel screams. It were Mary-Ellen and she'd seen her ring. She cried out that the ring were hers, and when Mrs Paget tries to part the two ladies, Mary-Ellen seized the big scissors lying on the counter, like this, "Give it to me, or I'll kill you!" '

Mrs Bean grabbed a fork and made a dramatic stabbing motion at her husband, and Fred, reeling back, cried, 'Don't do it, Elsie. I haven't finished me tea.'

Helpless laughter broke out round Eliot, but he was too caught up in Mary-Ellen's moment of fury to take part in it. 'She didn't, did she?' he asked gravely, 'didn't kill the woman?'

Mrs Bean frowned, having lost her thread. 'Kill her?' Eliot persisted. 'The scissors. She didn't kill her?'

'Goodness, no. Some of the customers pulled her away, got the scissors off her, I don't know the details. But after that they had to keep her at home. Locked in her room. Out of harm's way. Mr Flowers was a very stern gentleman. Very proud. He didn't want no one to see his daughter's . . . humiliation, if you like.'

'Did she go mad, then?' Violet asked.

Eliot thought of his room: the cracked mirror, the barred window.

'You could say that. She was better off at home, I can tell you. A madhouse in those days were a rum kind of place.' She glanced at the clock. 'I wouldn't like you to think we want to get rid of you, dears,' she said, 'but it's a long ride back to Saintbury, and time's getting on.'

They rose from the table and began to pile the crockery together. Mrs Bean tried to shoo them away, saying that she would deal with it in her own time, but the girls wouldn't listen. Eliot stood with his back to the window, aware of the great sweep of crops rustling behind him. And he felt an intense and mysterious tug, as though fingers that couldn't quite touch him were trying to reach him. 'You haven't told us about the second time,' he said, 'when Mary-Ellen was seen again. You said it was much, much worse.'

Violet and Noni looked round from the sink, and Violet turned off the jet of water. They waited expectantly for Mrs Bean to continue, but this time it was Fred who told them about a walk that he and Elsie had taken by the river, more than twenty years before. How they had reached the clump of willows, where the steps to the footbridge began. He described the boy as though he was seeing him still, in his yellow T-shirt and faded jeans, diving from the bank and striking out into the current, where he turned and turned, in such a frenzy they

60

thought he would drown from exhaustion.

'He kept calling, "Where is she? Where is she? Did you see? A woman fell off the bridge?" But we didn't see nothing 'cept him, did we, Elsie?'

Mrs Bean shook her head. She was almost as overcome now, as she had been then. Her husband had to continue. 'Quite a crowd had gathered by then, and we thought the lad would drown. He were a teenager really, a tall lad but the current's that strong by the bridge, and the river's deep. A man jumped in and pulled the boy to the bank; I helped to pull them both out. The boy was in a right state, shaking all over. But it was fright as much as cold. He wouldn't take a coat or tell us his name, just stumbled away. The man who saved him had his picture in the papers, but not the boy. No one ever found out who he was. Elsie had to sit on a bench to recover, and we stayed there, I don't know how long,' Fred glanced at his wife. 'She'd guessed what the boy had seen.'

'What?' begged Noni. 'What had he seen?'

'It were the same bridge, dear,' Mrs Bean said in a low voice, and she shrugged as though trying to shake off the memory. 'That's how Mary-Ellen did away with herself when she couldn't take no more. The river was full, so drowning was easy. She'd put aside her black, Nancy told me, and was wearing the dress she went out walking in, with her young man. Dove-grey. That's why I thought it were a swan the boy saw, a young one before it had grown its white feathers. But I knew in my heart that it wasn't. It was Midsummer's day, you see. The day Mary-Ellen drowned, nearly sixty years before.'

For a moment no one spoke. Violet turned the tap and began to fill the sink again while Noni and Eliot cleared the table.

'D'you believe in ghosts, then, Eliot?' asked Mrs Bean. She was taking an empty plate out of his hands and didn't look directly at him.

He said, 'Yes,' and she put her small hand over his and smiled. And there was something behind the smile that told him she had more to say, a secret that, one day, might belong to him.

When they left the farm the sun had dropped directly into their path, turning the fields into great sheets of silver. They rode with one hand up to shield their eyes, and their shadows streamed behind them, like ribbons of dark silk. They covered several miles without speaking and Eliot wondered if the day had meant anything at all to Violet and Noni. But when they dismounted to walk single file across the bridge into town, Violet suddenly said, 'Mum and Dad were here twenty years ago. Maybe they heard about the boy in the river.'

'So our house has quite a history,' said Sophie, as they were drinking their last cup of tea before bed. Between them, the girls had related Mary-Ellen's story.

'And are you using this for a history project, or what?' inquired the dentist, surreptitiously dropping half a teaspoonful of sugar into his tea.

'It's just good to know about the people who lived in your house,' said Noni, 'especially when something dramatic happens to them. There was a ghost, you know, seen twice. The second time a boy jumped into the river, just where Mary-Ellen drowned. It was over twenty years ago. Mrs Bean swears he must have seen the ghost. The river was high and the boy nearly drowned, but a man jumped in to save him. He had his picture in the paper, the man that is. The boy just disappeared. No one ever found out who he was.'

Sophie stared into her cup. 'We know who it was,' she said with a meaningful look at the dentist. He nodded back at her.

'Who?' asked Eliot, painfully alert.

'I don't see why you shouldn't know. We didn't tell anyone then because – he begged us not to, but now . . .' Sophie hesitated, then turning to Eliot, she said, 'It was your father, Eliot!'

7

Orlando Furioso

Noni and Violet looked at Eliot. Noni's mouth slid open but not a word came out. Violet frowned in consternation.

Eliot's mind reeled. Sophie's answer was so unexpected and, somehow, unwelcome. How could she say such a thing? It wasn't possible.

'Why?' he asked in a voice that seemed to gasp for air.

'Eliot, darling. Don't look so stricken. It happened a long time ago. There's nothing sinister about it. Gilbert nearly drowned, it's true. But he didn't. He lived a long and healthy life, married Lily . . . and . . .'

'Lily died!' cried Eliot.

He left the room. A voice, he couldn't tell whose, called out to him, but sounds were muffled. The pattern on the stair carpet swung under his feet as he felt Mary-Ellen draw closer. Closer and closer. Now he must include his father in the picture. Eliot had thought him far away, a safe person, beyond Mary-Ellen's reach. But she had already touched Gilbert.

In his room, the scent of flowers was overwhelming. Eliot tried to imagine how it would feel to be locked in there all day, all night. He counted the bars at the window. Eight. Mr Flowers could not afford the embarrassment of a daughter's tumble from the roof. So how had she managed to reach the river?

There was a distant rumble. A juggernaut perhaps was rolling down the High Street. The sound grew into a monotonous boom, more like a distant cannon than an engine. The pile of books on Eliot's bedside table rocked and tumbled to the floor. The lamp crashed over. His jacket slid off the bed. The sounds of thunder died but Eliot's room still trembled. Three framed prints clattered to the floor, their glass shattered, and as Eliot stood, more baffled than afraid, an object slid through the air towards him. He watched, in disbelief, its gravity-defying progress. *Orlando Furioso* was levelled at his head. Eliot ran to the door, wrenched it open and made for the stairs, but with horrible precision the book turned into the landing and followed him.

'Eliot, are you . . .?' Violet's anxious face stared up from the hall.

'No!' he yelled. The book had suddenly gained momentum; it swept down, like a bird of prey. The draught blew Violet's hair away from her face as the book slammed into her forehead. She dropped to the ground with a moan.

Eliot, stumbling downstairs, reached Violet at the same time as the others. She was holding her head, still conscious but mute with shock. Through the babble of exclamations, Eliot heard her whisper, 'Why?'

Sophie picked up the book. 'What happened?' she asked.

Noni said, 'You threw it, Eliot, didn't you?'

'No.'

Sophie, helping Violet to her feet, demanded, 'What's going on?'

'It came through the air,' Violet said. 'It wasn't meant to hit me. I just walked into it.' She rubbed her forehead. 'Ouch!'

'Books don't fly,' muttered Noni.

'You're going to have a bruise,' Sophie stroked Violet's hair back. 'How d'you feel. Dizzy? Can you focus properly?'

'Of course, Mum,' Violet said impatiently. 'Don't fuss, please!'

'Eliot, I want a word with you,' Sophie said.

'OK.'

She followed him upstairs. Too late, he remembered the state of his room. He heard Sophie's sharp intake of breath, but she tried to look calm as she surveyed the chaos. She picked up the lamp and stood it, carefully, on the bedside table. Then she sat on the bed, patting the quilt beside her. Eliot perched on the edge and regarded the fragments of glass along the wainscot. Was he supposed to apologise?

'I don't know what happened,' he said. 'Something outside, a tanker maybe, passing in the street, shook everything in the room. And then the book just came at me.'

'How did you feel when all this started? Were you angry about something?'

'No.' He glanced at her quickly.

'We mentioned your mother. Maybe it upset you?'

He shook his head.

'Perhaps we should talk a bit more about this, Eliot.'

'No,' he said vehemently. 'Dad said put the past behind you. He's right.'

'Would you like to see your father for a few days?'

Eliot stared at her. 'It wasn't me,' he said. 'It was *her*. You know – *her*! Dad's got nothing to do with it.'

Sophie bit her lip. 'You might like to talk to him,' she said gently. 'He could pop up on Friday night, go for a walk with you, stay a couple of nights, be gone on Sunday.'

'I don't have anything to tell him,' Eliot insisted. And yet, of course, he did. But would his father admit to seeing Mary-Ellen, or had he shut her away, best-forgotten, like Lily?

Sophie went over to the fallen pictures and propped them against the wall. One pane of glass was still intact. 'A bonus,' she said, ruefully. 'You'd better come and get a dustpan and brush, and some newspaper to wrap up the broken glass. Perhaps Noni will help you.'

'Sophie!' Eliot's voice stopped her at the door. 'Please, believe me. I didn't mean to hurt anyone.'

'I know, Eliot. But Violet *was* hurt, and I must make sure that doesn't happen again.' She spoke with a crisp sort of kindness that wasn't entirely sympathetic.

'It wasn't me . . .' he murmured as she went away.

The house was very quiet. Sudden rage had drained Eliot's room of energy. The air seemed lifeless, the scent of flowers too faint to identify. Eliot lay back, wearily, his arms folded behind his neck. He felt too exhausted to sweep up the broken glass. He gazed at the ceiling where a circle of reflected light shimmered hazily. One side of the ring was broken by a cluster of blue and crimson flames. He had become so accustomed to the sign, he merely asked, 'Can't you let it go? You're hurting people!'

'No,' he answered for her. 'You can't. You're desperate. I guess I'll have to go and get it for you.' He fell asleep, hardly realising what he had said.

July 1917

Mary-Ellen lies on her narrow bed. She has a new room, a small space on the top floor where the maid used to sleep. They have barred her window and locked the door. She sees no one except Ada, the nurse, a strong country girl who can wrestle her to the floor when she has to.

Every morning Ada slides a tray of food inside the door, then locks it quickly. But Mary-Ellen hasn't thrown a thing for days. At first she used any object she could hurl: a hairbrush, a shoe, a pillow, a spoon. And when poor Ada came for the empty plate she would get that, too, smashed against the door when she opened it, or a glass of water in the face. Once a small fruit knife had been the missile, not sharp but slim and dangerous all the same. They don't give Mary Ellen knives any more. The food arrives in bite-sized cubes. It isn't appetising. She drops the food, crumb by crumb through the bars of her window. She has lost a stone in weight, but she doesn't have to suffer her wasting reflection. Last week she smashed her mirror with a paperweight. They took the mirror away. A tiny slither of glass is hidden in Mary Ellen's drawer. They missed that. One day she will use it.

No one will listen to her. That's all she wants, to keep Orlando with her, to keep alive his laughter, his footsteps at her side, his grace, his marvellous dark eyes, his gentleness.

'Dead!' they tell her. 'Gone! Nothing of him left!' They are denying what's in her head. 'Let it go, Mary-Ellen. The past is dead!' Not so.

'People die,' they say. A bomb fell on London and killed her mother's sister, Auntie Maud. No one expected it. The zeppelins were easy to shoot down, but not the nippy little German aeroplanes. Boom! Boom! They dropped their bombs and were gone.

Her father stands outside her door, sometimes, and lectures her on facing up to things, on wicked wastage. The King himself has cut consumption of bread and potatoes. The royal household goes two days a week without meat. 'Poor things!' Nancy Dove would say in her funny, hungry little voice.

Mary-Ellen's mother stands outside her door and weeps and prays.

The evenings are worse. They won't give her a candle. That's understandable, of course. She would set alight the bed. Anything to warm her spirits.

She keeps the book he gave her under her pillow, where her hand can find it, even while she sleeps.

Orlando Furioso. She takes it out and for the hundredth time gazes at the pictures of knights in armour, monsters and demons, the Emperor Charlemagne. Her finger traces the outline of the hero, Orlando, mad with fury over Angelica, his faithless love.

'I am not faithless, Orlando. We will always be one. Always.' She sees again the circling ocean of wheat as their bodies met and spun. In the distance a cloud of birds sweeps over the roof of Dove Farm, their wings blazing white in the sun.

'A dance, Miss Flowers?'

'Signor Orlando, of course!'

'Do you love me, Mary-Ellen?'

'Always and forever.'

Their last day together. But now she must have the ring to keep faith with him. Why can't they understand?

A key moves in the lock. Mary-Ellen sits up, straightening her skirt. She frowns at the opening door and her father walks in. Ada is two steps behind – just in case.

'I've come to make you an offer,' he says.

'I want my ring!'

'That's foolishness.' He dismisses her need with an impatient gesture. 'We think you're well enough to join us for supper. Would you like that, Mary-Ellen?'

She slides bare feet on to the floor and stands rigid beside the bed. 'I want my ring.' Her voice is harsh, almost a scream. Ada moves further into the room. 'It's mine. Don't you understand? Freya got it under false pretences, buried my engagement as though it were dead.'

'Child, it *is* dead. The ring is hers now. Oliviero gave it to her. Let it go.'

'N-o-o-o-o-O!' She swings *Orlando Furioso* at the greying head.

Mr Flowers ducks, as much from the awful howl, as from the book that comes hurtling towards him. Ada leaps and misses. *Orlando Furioso* is a marvel. He flies over their heads, through the open door and up, up, up, his feathery pages like the wings of an angel.

'Orlando!' cries Mary-Ellen laughing delightedly. She is still laughing when the book slams into Mrs Flowers running up the stairs. There is a cry of pain, a bump, a moan.

Mr Flowers' large hand cuts across Mary Ellen's cheek. 'Wicked girl!'

She is alone again, in the locked room.

8

The headstone

The dentist, back from a two-hour jog, brought an air of calm to the uneasy household. Eliot, sitting opposite Violet at supper, noted the bruise above her left eye. She had tried, unsuccessfully, to hide it with a lock of hair. The dentist didn't allude to her mishap. They had obviously decided not to speak of it in front of him, fearing another outburst, perhaps?

That night he listened for the phantom marchers, dreading the sound, yet almost disappointed when they didn't come. They were ghosts now, all of them. Had any returned from the war? Who would remember? There was bound to be a memorial somewhere in the town. Their names would be on it. He would ask Violet or Noni to come with him, after school on Monday.

It hadn't occurred to Eliot that the girls would feel nervous in his company. But when he begged them to come Noni said firmly, 'You can find the memorial yourself, Eliot. It's in the square at the top of the town, between the two churches. You can't miss it!'

'D'you think I'll find Orlando's name there?'

'How should I know?' Noni was very offhand.

'Why d'you want to find his name?' Violet asked gently.

He considered his answer, not really sure what it would be. 'It's a starting point,' he said. 'I know Orlando existed, because Mrs Bean said so, but I just want to see his name for myself. Maybe it'll tell me something about Mary-Ellen.'

'What?' said Noni. 'What could it tell you? We know about Mary-Ellen. We know she lived here, once. Finding Orlando won't prove that she's still – about.'

'I know,' said Eliot, with a guilty glance at Violet's bruise. 'But I've got to do *something*. I guess I'll do it right now.'

His impatience with them made him leap from the table. He couldn't stand the furtive looks they darted at him. He left the house, slamming the door behind him.

It was true. The memorial wasn't difficult to find. As he ascended the final curving road to the two churches, the great cross suddenly came into view. It seemed to look out over the town with what Eliot felt to be a reproving gaze. He walked past St Mary's, the Roman Catholic church, but just as he passed the lychgate he caught sight of a blond head, bobbing behind a stone cross. Someone evidently didn't want to be seen. Eliot wondered why. Instead of going straight up to the memorial, Eliot turned into St Mary's graveyard. A boy in a blue anorak was kneeling by a headstone. When he saw Eliot he jumped up and ran off, weaving between the graves and finally disappearing behind the grey bulk of the church.

Curious, Eliot walked over to the place where the boy

had been kneeling. He found something startling: a bunch of sweet rocket, loosely tied with white ribbons. The name on the headstone was puzzling. Oliviero Carlo Rinaldi. Another Rinaldi. Could there be two, or had the Beans mistaken this name for Orlando? Impossible. There was *Orlando Furioso* to bear witness. Eliot read on: '*Last surviving son of Roberto Giulio Rinaldi and Alicia Sophia Rinaldi. Born, September 1897. Died April, 1918. A Victim of the Great War.*'

Eliot stepped back. All the details fitted, except the name. And was it merely a coincidence that someone had placed here the flowers whose scent filled his room, and even followed him? He had a strong compulsion to touch the flowers, but a presence hovered in the graveyard, a chilly wind that crept across his skull. He backed away from the grave, then turned, ran through the gate and didn't stop until he stood beside the gaunt memorial.

There were so many names. Eliot thrust his cold hands in his pockets and began to read from the top of the first column. The wind whipped his legs and pulled strands of hair into his eyes. He kept losing his place and having to scan the names again. But there it was, between Ridley and Robertson. Rinaldi, Orlando Gaetano. No flowers here. So who had been tending the grave at St Mary's? Who was Oliviero? Eliot retraced his steps. He was so distracted he almost walked into the woman who came through the lychgate: Freya Greymark.

She wore a black coat and a mauve hat pulled over her tough grey hair. In one black-gloved hand, she held the bunch of sweet rocket. Eliot knew they were the same by the tendrils of white ribbon that flapped in the wind. Her yellow eyes glared into his, but it was Eliot who spoke first.

'You've stolen those flowers. They're not yours.' Brave words when his skin prickled under her gaze.

'What do you know about it?' Her voice was reedy with annoyance.

'It's wrong. Messing with someone else's grave.'

'Be quiet!' She whirled away, so fast and unexpectedly, Eliot was too stunned to move. Inside the gate a trail of tiny flower-heads led across the grass, where she had ripped them from their stalks. By the time he had gathered enough courage to chase after her, she had rounded a corner – and vanished. But strolling along the other side of the road, was the boy Eliot had seen in the graveyard.

'Hi!' called Eliot.

The boy glanced up and then took flight, his skinny legs racing down hill with desperate toppling leaps.

'Slow down,' cried Eliot, now in pursuit. 'I only want to talk.'

The other boy took a corner and, almost as soon as he disappeared, there was a sudden, high wail. Following the sound, Eliot turned into a narrow, tree-lined avenue. The boy sat sprawled across the pavement right in front of him.

'This is your fault,' said the boy, drawing up his knees. His jeans were streaked with mud and dust. 'Ouch!' he grunted.

'Why d'ya take off like that?' Eliot demanded. 'I wasn't gonna eat you.'

'Huh!' mumbled the boy. 'You saw me with the flowers. You were going to have a good laugh.'

'No. I swear.' Eliot squatted beside the boy, who seemed about his age. 'I wasn't even sure it was you who'd put the flowers there. I was following someone else.'

'Who?'

'A woman in a black coat. She took your flowers.'

The boy looked alarmed. 'Why?' he asked.

'That's what I'd like to know.'

'D'you think I'll have to do it all over again, get more flowers, I mean? I hate doing it! But if no one knows it won't matter, will it?' he added hopefully. Eliot wished he hadn't mentioned the flowers.

'It's OK,' he said. 'No one's gonna know unless they go there regularly. And I'm sure not gonna tell anyone.'

'Thanks.' The boy heaved a sigh. 'You're American, aren't you?'

'Only half. Dad's British. My name's Eliot.'

'I'm Sam,' the boy gave his name a little grudgingly. 'Were you looking for an ancestor back there?' He began to brush his jeans with grubby fingers.

Eliot shook his head.

'Who, then?'

Eliot drew a breath. 'It's hard to explain. I was looking for a soldier called Rinaldi. But not the one whose name is on the headstone. It's not a regular kind of name for an English person, so were they related? What's the story about the sweet rocket?'

The boy darted him a suspicious look. 'Why d'you want to know?'

'You'll laugh.'

'Try me.'

Eliot felt he couldn't handle a long explanation, so he said, rather defiantly, 'I'm being haunted.'

Sam's reaction was surprising. No laugh, just a widening of his eyes. He stood up and frowned at the grazed palms of his hands. 'I bet it's Mary-Ellen.' He gave Eliot a grim smile.

'How the heck . . .?' Eliot got to his feet, searching the boy's face.

'She seems to haunt our family, well, Auntie Nancy, anyway. Auntie Nancy's really old. She can't walk far any more, so she pays me to do the flowers. She had this friend, Mary-Ellen, years and years ago. Well, Mary-Ellen's fiancé died in the First World War, and she always put flowers on his grave. But then Mary-Ellen died, so Auntie Nancy did the flowers for her. They have to be those pale purply ones, don't ask me why. In the evening they smell really strong – it sort of hangs about, that smell, doesn't it?'

'Nancy,' Eliot murmured. 'Who is Nancy? Someone told me about a Nancy who'd seen a ghost. Mr Bean and his wife. Fred Bean.'

'Uncle Fred,' said Sam. 'I'm related to loads of people round here. I think Uncle Fred knew Mary-Ellen too, but she was really special to Auntie Nancy. She saw Mary-Ellen's ghost outside a house in our road.'

'Your road?' Eliot began to remember where he'd seen the boy before.

'Salter Row. The ghost was crying on Miss Greymark's doorstep. I saw you there, too, just a few days ago, didn't I?'

'You know Miss Greymark, then?' Eliot exclaimed. 'She was the one who took your flowers.'

'Hell!' said Sam. 'Why did she do that? She's gruesome that woman. Even Mum's afraid of her.'

'What I want to know is, why *that* grave? Orlando was Mary-Ellen's fiancé and he never came back from the war. No bones, no body. He was just . . . missing. That's why his name's on the memorial. So who's this other guy, this Oliviero?'

'I just do the flowers,' Sam said defensively. 'I don't spend time reading the names.'

'Damn it, what's the reason for it?' Eliot spoke almost to himself. He had an idea. 'Could I see this Auntie Nancy?'

'What for?'

'To talk to. I'm not in school right now. I've kinda left for a while . . .'

'Why?'

'None of your business.' He regretted that. 'Sorry,' he said. 'It's just that I've got time, too much, really.'

Sam gave him a look that was both envious and suspicious.

'So could I?' Eliot pressed. 'Could you set it up for me?'

'I s'pose. She's old. Over ninety.'

'But not . . . forgetful or funny or anything?'

'Nope. I'll take you there now if you like. She gives me a quid for doing the flowers.' He began to walk away.

'Sure, I'd like,' said Eliot leaping to the other boy's side.

Sam's aunt lived in Saddle Street, a continuation of Fly Street, once you crossed the main road.

'She lives alone,' Sam explained, 'but she has carers, twice a week, and my mum does her heavy shopping.' He opened a gate and led Eliot along a neatly bordered path.

The house was a two-storey semi-detached, a square building coated in pebble-dash. The ground floor windows were curtained in thick cream-coloured net. 'She sleeps downstairs,' Sam said, and rang the bell.

A few seconds later the door was opened by a cheerful-looking woman in a pink jogging suit.

'Hullo, Mrs Horner,' Sam said quickly. 'Can I see my aunt?'

'Oh, Sam, love, your auntie's asleep.' Mrs Horner lowered her voice. 'She's not too well. Had a little turn yesterday. She'll be laid up for a week or two.'

'Laid up,' Eliot exclaimed. 'She's not going to . . .'

'This is Eliot,' Sam explained. 'He wants to talk to Auntie Nancy.'

'What about?' the woman asked, frowning.

Eliot couldn't think how to put it. 'About the past,' he said weakly.

'Can't someone else help you, dear?'

Sam glanced quickly at Eliot who tried to look hopeful and failed. 'No,' Sam said. 'Because it's got something to do with the flowers. You know, the ones we have to take to the dead soldier in the cemetery. Eliot's sort of related to him.' He told this lie with assurance. 'He's from America.'

'Really?' Mrs Horner's expression changed

immediately. 'How interesting. Mrs Rose wouldn't like to miss an opportunity like this . . . but, Eliot, I daren't let her have a visitor yet. Doctor's orders. Come round this time next week, and if she's . . . well, I'll see what I can do.'

'Thanks.' Eliot felt bitterly disappointed. He stared at the impenetrable lace curtains. All at once, it had become vital for him to meet the old lady who slept behind them.

'Goodbye, then.' Mrs Horner threw Eliot an anxious glance and closed the door.

'It's not like Auntie Nancy,' Sam murmured, frowning. 'She always wants to see me. Slips me a fiver sometimes.'

'Is that the reason for your visits?'

'Well . . .' Sam grinned. 'It helps. But I like her a lot. She's not fussy, like some old people. She knows what's going on. She laughs at my jokes and . . . I can trust her.'

As they walked back to the main road, Eliot glanced ahead and saw a tall figure slip into a side street. She gave a brief shrivelling look before she disappeared. He knew it was meant for him.

'That creepy woman's everywhere,' he said. 'Maybe she uses stolen flowers for black magic rituals.'

'I don't want to know,' Sam said. 'Sometimes when I see her across the street, I can feel her hating everyone. She has a closed-up sort of face. Never smiles. When she was a teenager her mother fell downstairs and never walked again. Miss Greymark had to look after her until she died.'

'Then I guess that's why she's bitter. Sam, I've got to see your aunt,' Eliot suddenly exclaimed. 'It's real urgent. You don't think she'll die, do you?'

Sam stood still. 'She's lasted so long,' he hesitated. 'I thought she'd go on forever.'

And she knows, thought Eliot. She can go back years and years, to when it all began. And he felt as though the key to everything he needed was slipping out of reach. Sam's Auntie Nancy had known Mary-Ellen before she became a drifting, restless spirit. She had seen the real girl, before she lost her soldier and her precious ring. Perhaps she even knew why Mary-Ellen had chosen to haunt him, why he could hear the voice at this moment rasping inside his ear: 'Please! Get it.'

9
The falcon

They walked back to Fly Street together, before Sam made his way to Salter Row. 'See you in a week, then,' he called to Eliot as he took off.

'Before then, maybe!' Eliot was thinking of Freya Greymark's forbidding black door. Plans raced in his head. How could he get the ring? Would he have to climb a drainpipe, steal out at midnight? 'Maybe tomorrow,' he shouted. 'I want to take a look at Miss Greymark's place.'

'School for me,' groaned Sam as he took a corner and disappeared.

Eliot stepped into the Pipers' house and found it noisier than the street. Sophie's printer whirred to his left, the electric mixer to his right. Someone had the television on, and upstairs a hairdryer competed with a rock band. The sounds surrounded and excluded him. For a moment he didn't know where to go. At length he chose the kitchen.

Violet laid aside her whisk and switched it off. 'Your witch has just been here,' she said.

'Miss Greymark?'

'Uh-huh!'

'What did she want?' His heart thumped. Had she come to complain about him.

'Flowers,' said Violet. 'Sweet rocket, to be precise.'

Why would she steal them from a grave when there were so many in the gardens now?

' "You promised flowers," she said when Mum opened the door. "*Hesperis Matronalis*!" and she marched right through the house and out into our garden. Mum said, "Surely, it's not the time," but she rushed at the sweet rocket and snatched at the stalks like some greedy predator. Mum ran to get the clippers because the woman was tearing them out by the roots. It was horrible. She seemed so hungry for them, but she had no love for them at all. It was almost as if she were trying to kill them.'

'Did she take them all?' he asked.

'No. Mum stopped her. She had to be very firm though, had to shout at Miss Greymark to get through to her. She flew off with this great armful, without a thank-you or anything. She's a nasty piece of work.'

He told her about Nancy's promise to Mary-Ellen, about Sam, and the flowers the woman had stolen from a grave – a Rinaldi grave. And that would indicate that Freya Greymark's actions were very deliberate, that she was not only strange but evil. 'The Beans never mentioned that Orlando had a brother, did they?' he said. 'Nothing that sounded like Oliver?'

'No,' Violet said cheerfully. 'It's a mystery. By the way, I've been doing some research for you.'

'Research?' Intrigued, he sat down.

'I didn't set out to,' she admitted. 'I was doing my homework, a piece about myths, and the book fell open at a page I must have seen a dozen times but took no notice of. Only, this time I saw the name Freya, and I thought, let's look her up . . .'

'And . . .'

'She was this goddess of love, fertility and death. She wept tears of gold and listen, this is the best bit, she sometimes wore a falcon's skin.'

He thought of the yellowish eyes and the winging swoop towards him, the hawk on the black door. 'A falcon,' he murmured.

'Mysterious, eh?' Violet's grey eyes were alight.

'And was this goddess a thief?' he asked, thinking of the ring on Freya's finger. 'I mean, does a ring come into her story?'

'Mm. Don't think so. But she had a passion for jewels. Have a look for yourself.'

'I will.' Another book. Another story. He glanced at Violet's pale face and thought her more like Snow White than ever. Not the girl with the seven dwarfs but the one who was Rose Red's sister in the story that Lily read to him when he was very small. The kind and helpful Snow White who looked after a bear. He seemed to be caught in a web of stories, some of them true. 'Violet,' he said, 'it was *Orlando Furioso* that came flying at you.'

'Yes.' She was measuring sugar into a bowl and didn't look at him.

'I didn't throw the book. Someone else did.'

'Mary-Ellen?' She looked up.

'Who else. Something that happened all those years ago is starting up again. And I seem to have caused it. Like setting a match to paper. I'm scared.'

Violet was a girl who always tried hard to be helpful and say the right thing. Hoping it would sound like friendly advice, she said, 'Perhaps you can stop it. If you try.'

'I *can't*.' He stood up, angrily. 'You don't believe me, do you? You think all this trouble is coming from inside of me, because of . . .' His mother's name lay out of reach, far away in a different world. 'You're just humouring me. Nice, kind Snow White.' He stormed up to his room, trying to wish away the thunder in his head.

When he closed the door on the rest of the house, he slipped into the past so swiftly, he could almost feel the slither of familiar objects changing their structure under his hands. The wooden bed-frame hardened into cold metal. Cupboards shifted, rose and fell, the crisp gingham curtain that he grasped for comfort billowed under his touch, dark and velvety. He sank to the floor beneath the barred window, and watched *her* take shape.

She was sitting on a stool only a few feet away from him. Her black hair was a tempest of curls, there was so much of it, the tresses of a mad woman. Her eyes glittered darker even than her hair, wild and anguished. He hoped she would say something at last, but she merely lifted her pale left hand towards him. Her slender ringless fingers drooped; the gesture of a fairytale princess.

'I will get it,' he said. 'I promise.'

She leaned closer, peering into the corner where he sat. Eliot felt as though his heart had stopped.

Slowly she melted into the background and he closed his eyes against the heaving and sliding that took place as walls and furniture resumed the shapes he knew.

He was so shaken by the wild apparition, he couldn't move. He sat where he was until cool evening entered his room. There was a call for supper which he answered with a mumbled, 'Not hungry. Thanks!'

Sophie opened the door and frowned at him, crouched under the window. 'Aren't you well, Eliot? What is it?' She switched on the light and he cupped a hand over his eyes to shield them from the sudden glare.

'I'm OK,' he murmured. But his voice sounded so distant he wondered if she could hear him. 'I think I'll take a walk.'

'It's getting dark.'

'Just half an hour. It'll make me feel better.'

'Don't go too far, Eliot, please. I don't really think you should. Perhaps one of the girls . . .'

'No,' he said, getting to his feet. 'I'll just run to the end of the road and back. That's all. To get some air.' He had pins and needles from crouching so long, and had to disguise his cramped walk with the swaying strides of a clown.

'We'll save you some chips,' Sophie said.

It was still light outside. But he needed darkness, a few shadows to cover him. He thought of calling on Sam and asking him to keep watch, but decided it was unfair to include him in such a risky operation.

First he would have to find the back of Freya's house. This wasn't as difficult as he thought it would be. A narrow alley ran between the walled gardens of Salter Row and neighbouring Simpson Street. The walls of the Salter Row houses were six feet high and had wooden doors set into them. Each door was marked with a number. Eliot put his eye to a crack in the door of number seven. He saw a hopeless tangle of wild grass and brambles. Any flowers would have been smothered in such a jungle. But there was a small clearing in the centre where someone had placed a dustbin with several holes puncturing its rusty metal. An incinerator. Smoke steamed from the holes and from the open top; the reek of burning plants was nauseous. It filled Eliot's nostrils with the choking stench of some smouldering, exotic incense.

The fire at the base of the bin had not yet burned through to the layer of plants at the top. Some of them hung from the rim, a sprinkling of tiny petals, like pale violet stars.

Freya Greymark was burning sweet rocket.

She came through a door at the back of the house and her tall figure startled Eliot into leaping back from his post. But, certain she couldn't see him beyond the high wall, he pressed his face to the door again. She was pushing the flowers down into the bin with a long hoe, leaning on the shaft with a ferocious determination. Smoke billowed round her and she spat into the undergrowth as if she were ridding herself of poison.

Eliot stepped back, his eyes smarting from the stench.

He wondered why the neighbours weren't shouting out complaints. Was everyone afraid of Freya Greymark? I can't afford to be, he thought. I have to go in there. It seemed such a reckless enterprise, he marvelled at his own persistence. But, of course, Mary-Ellen would be with him every step of the way. He couldn't refuse her now. Her fingertips were on his sleeve, her small knuckles at his back. Insisting.

Was it fate that made Freya leave the back door ajar? Or was it a draught that slipped through the latch before it caught? The door in the wall was easy. He turned a handle and it swung inwards, half-rotten with damp. Eliot made his way through the tangle of undergrowth. Smoke hung in the garden and drifted in pale threads about his head. He put a hand over his mouth to stop the cough that burned the back of his throat.

Up three steps and into a dark passage. Something at the other end rustled into a garment. The falcon skin? The front door opened and it hopped out, stirring the air with its dark wings, its yellow-rimmed eyes probing the street. The door slammed behind its sudden flight. Whatever it was, woman or bird, it was gone. And Eliot was free to search for the ring.

He should have gone upstairs, into a bedroom, where precious things are kept: bracelets, rings, necklaces and earrings. But Eliot made the mistake of beginning his search in the living-room, where a collection of photographs held his attention.

They hung on the wall in a group; six sepia-tinted, black-framed photographs, each one neatly captioned at the bottom in expert calligraphy. They formed part of the story that Eliot was trapped in. He began with the top left picture, as though the group comprised the page of a graphic novel. It was a studio portrait of two people: the girl was tall with cropped blonde hair, the man much older. He wore a pin-striped suit and the chain of his fob-watch hung across a tight-fitting waistcoat. The caption read, *Freya Simnel and Arthur Greymark 1924*. Next came a wedding photograph of the unlikely couple. *St Barnabas 1925*. Eliot passed on to picture number three: the same couple sitting on a brocade-covered sofa. A blonde baby was cradled on her mother's knee. *1930*.

The next photograph had been taken several years later. The mother was in black, she had filled out considerably and looked coarse and solid. The girl, so clearly her daughter, leaned her pale head on the broad shoulder. *Freya and little Freya 1935*. There was a change of scene in the picture beside it: a garden where the mother sat in a wheelchair, morose and defeated. She did not even attempt a smile. Her hands were neatly folded, her gaze drawn to something beyond the camera lens. Already looking for heaven. The girl stood behind her mother, her fingers resting on the draped shoulders, and a kind of rage had grown in the girl's eye. The muscles of her face were set, her nose protruded beak-like from the hollows beneath her eyes, and her pallid flesh was pulled taut over the high cheekbones. *1943*.

The last picture seemed to have no place in the group. The caption read *Lt Oliver Rinaldi 1917*. The man who lay in the graveyard. He was in uniform, dark and handsome as Eliot would have expected, and he had a winning smile. And yet it was not the face of a man Mary-Ellen would want to remember with flowers. The eyes were remote and slightly cunning. Why was it hanging with Freya Greymark's family?

Eliot stepped away from the photographs, the better to study them as a collection. He perched on the arm of a chair, hardly aware he was doing so. Dusk slid into the house and a chill draught. The room of heavy furniture and cold grey colours enclosed him in a mysterious gloom. The story set out before him took on a sinister aspect. Each face was tinged with some unpleasant feature: they sneered and raged at him, their hatred personal, and Eliot felt stunned by the force of their antagonism. It was almost as if they thought him someone else.

'Mary-Ellen,' he murmured.

He was still under their spell when a hawk-like figure swept up Salter Row. He didn't see her pass the netted window. But she stopped on the step, frowned, listened and peered close to the pane, her sharp eyes narrowing.

Sam, watching the street from his bedroom window, saw the dark figure perched on her step. He saw her stretch her long neck towards the windowpane and with a sudden flash of intuition, he knew that Eliot was in the house, in danger.

Slowly, Freya Greymark put her key into the lock, turned it and pushed the door ajar. She inched stealthily inside, and the black door closed without a sound.

Eliot didn't even sense her presence. But when she spoke he felt his pulse stop and wondered if he'd died of fright.

'What a wicked boy it is. What shall we do with it? Evil, snooping child.'

He turned a stunned face towards her. Excuses sprang to mind, too pathetic to utter. So he just stood up, wretchedly, with his mouth hanging open, waiting for whatever words might find their way on to his tongue.

'Who are you?' The hawk's eyes glinted.

'I'm from . . .'

'Oh, I know all about that.' She made an impatient gesture. 'I mean what's behind all this prying . . . all this persecution.'

'I haven't . . .'

'Sit down! Go on. Sit!' Eliot fell back into the chair. 'You want to know about them?' She pointed at the photographs. 'Well, I'll tell you and then you can go away with some understanding of my tragedy. Perhaps I'll never know why you've been chosen to hound me, perhaps you won't either.'

'I'm not a dog,' Eliot spoke up at last. 'I'm not hounding you.'

'Shut up!' she snapped. 'You sit there and listen, and then you can go. Never let me see you again. Not once . . . ever.'

'Why?' he asked in a half-whisper.

'You bring a stench with you. You carry something,' she glanced over his shoulder, 'unpleasant. Something I'm trying to get rid of, entirely. For my mother's sake.'

'You're like your mother.' He glanced at the photographs, feeling bolder.

'Yes,' she said, almost pleased with his observation. 'Yes, I am my mother. We have become one. I want you to hear her story because I believe that, for one reason or another, your sympathy has been misplaced. And this bothers me.'

'I just wandered into this,' he said. 'I'm not connected to these dead people in any way.'

'I think you are.' She took a chair opposite his and leaned close, her gaze flickering round his head and shoulders as though she were printing his shape in her mind.

'No . . . it's impossible, I'm just staying in a house where things happened. I've got nothing to do with them. Nothing.'

'Listen,' she said. 'You see that man?' She pointed at the photograph of Oliver Rinaldi. 'He gave my mother a ring – the Rinaldi ring. An heirloom from his family. He wanted her to have it. They were to be married.'

'But wasn't Orlando . . .?' Words failed him, his mouth felt dry and uncomfortable.

'Listen,' she hissed. 'Oliver, that's what my mother and I called him, though it was really Oliviero. Oliver had a brother, yes. His name was Orlando and yes, he was the elder of the two. He died in France a few days before Oliver went missing.

'Orlando gave the Rinaldi ring to Mary-Ellen Flowers,' Eliot declared. 'So how come Oliver got hold of it?'

'His father passed it on to him,' she replied dismissively.

'No,' he muttered.

'Yes!' She pushed herself out of the chair and loomed over him.

'It's a lie,' he murmured, frightened of the mad look in her eyes. But he couldn't lose faith with Mary-Ellen. He knew that Mrs Bean had told the true story and, glancing at the cunning face of Oliver Rinaldi, he also knew something else, and made himself brave enough to say it. 'Your mother's boyfriend stole the ring.'

He could feel the ache she had to hit him, or dig her talons into his neck, but she backed off a little and breathed, 'How dare you?' And then she poured out a story, aiming words at Eliot like arrows.

'When my mother was twenty-one, a young man came into her life, his name was Oliviero Rinaldi. His family were Italian; bakers and confectioners. Eventually, they built the Grand Hotel.' Eliot had seen it, a tall red-brick building with a glass verandah running the length of the first floor; an elegant structure, grand but beautiful. 'It's where they met, Oliver and Freya, my mother. Orlando and Mary-Ellen would be there, at the dances. Mary-Ellen was only seventeen and so precocious. Her hair had a life of its own, my mother said, unruly, never pinned up properly. She would show off in a most unbecoming way, wild and foolish. Her arms round Orlando's neck, her eyes on fire.

'Orlando was the favourite son. Poor Oliver always got second best. There was a year between them but they both joined up together in 1917, both officers. They looked like twins.' No, thought Eliot, they were not the same at all.

'Orlando gave Mary-Ellen a ring, the Rinaldi ring, and they were engaged, officially. But Oliver had to wait, Mr Rinaldi had a grudge against my mother. She wasn't good enough for them, but foolish Mary-Ellen won his heart. Well, the war put a stop to all that. Her precious Orlando was blown to smithereens, not a shred left.'

Eliot had never heard anyone speak so coldly of another person's death. He had to hug himself to keep warm. 'Grey skies are better than cold hearts,' his father had said. But here was a heart of ice. Freya seemed to enjoy his distress. 'Little Mary-Ellen lost her place,' she said. 'And my mother got the Rinaldi ring.'

'Wait,' begged Eliot. 'You can't take back something that has already been given. It was Mary-Ellen's ring forever.'

'No!'

Eliot tightened his arms round himself, but he couldn't feel the edges of his body; all his senses were under threat from her eyes. The dark room spun, the furniture dissolved in clouds about him. I'm going to faint, he thought, and then what will she do? Because she's not a normal person at all.

He could still hear her voice, droning insistently into his ears. 'It was Oliver's ring and he gave it to my mother, poor Freya. And Oliver came home from the war all broken up, poor boy. So horribly maimed, he didn't want to live. My mother went to see him, just the once, and then he died. An overdose of morphine. No one inquired how or why. It was obvious. A year later Mary-Ellen threw herself off the Saintbury bridge. She was quite mad by then, should have been locked up. Then Freya, my mother, married Mr Greymark. Nice, respectable, a lot older of course, but safe. My father. He died when I was five. My mother took to wearing the Rinaldi ring again; it was hers.'

Eliot couldn't argue. The world around him had lost its shape. He thought: I suppose I'm hypnotised.

Back came the voice, a thread of words trickling into his head. 'The haunting started when I was eight. First she just came to the door, weeping and calling out. I thought it was the wind, but my mother said, "No. It's Mary-Ellen. She wants my ring." Sometimes, my mother would curl her fingers into a fist, to stop the girl from snatching her treasure. She could feel the nails, she said, tearing at her knuckles.

'I only saw her once, and it was the worst day of my life. It was wartime again. 1941. There was an air-raid warning, bombs coming our way, doodlebugs they called them. My mother was at the top of the stairs. "Run to the shelter, little Freya," she said. She always called me little Freya. "I'll be there soon. I'll just fetch another candle."

'Something made me turn back: an ill wind, the smell of disaster. I saw my mother edging away from her door. She backed towards the stairs. I called out, "Mother, take care." But it was too late. She fell. I'll never forget it. I couldn't do anything to stop the awful tumble. She landed at my feet, still conscious but broken, ruined. "Is she still there?" Mother whispered, and I looked up, shaking, my candle bouncing shadows all around me, and I saw a girl at the top of the staircase, a mad creature with a mass of wild hair, and the crushing scent of her made me feel ill. Sweet rocket.'

'She didn't mean to hurt,' Eliot whispered. 'Your mother was punished by her guilty conscience.' He was given these words by a voice in his head, but he spoke them as if they were his.

'Stupid boy,' Freya snarled. 'Who are you to know?'

He was about to answer when he realised that he wasn't quite sure any more. So he just said, 'I think I'll go home now, they'll be worried.'

'Perhaps they'll think you've run away again,' she said. 'I know all about that, you see. I've been asking questions, a bit of a runner, aren't you?'

All at once the Pipers' home seemed such a safe place. He badly wanted to be there, surrounded by people who knew who he was and cared about what happened to him. 'So I'd better get back there, hadn't I?' he said.

'I've changed my mind.' Her voice was steely. 'You would do better to stay here with me, until we get to the root of this . . . this wickedness, and then we can snuff it out. Can't we, Eliot?'

'What are you talking about?' he tried to get up but his legs wouldn't support him and he toppled back with a whimper.

Her tall frame came so close he could hear the grinding of sinews under her coarse grey clothes. 'I'm not letting you go until we find out who you really are,' she said. 'They'll just assume you've done a bunk again, won't they?'

10

A spear of glass

Sam tidied his homework into a drawer and ran downstairs. 'Going to get a magazine,' he called out. His mother murmured something from the kitchen as he left the house. He ran across the road to number seven and waited on the step, listening. He could hear Miss Greymark's strange, monotonous voice. She droned like an insect. Something told him that his new friend was in danger.

Sam peered at the net curtains, the drone increasing as he got closer. He could just make out Eliot's bright T-shirt. Sam enjoyed mysteries; he usually had to invent them, but here was a real one almost on his own doorstep. Rescuing Eliot was going to be difficult. Distracting Miss Greymark was the only solution. If Sam knocked, Eliot could make his escape when she came to the door.

He looked up at the brass hawk. The glare of its shiny eye seemed all too lifelike. He put his hand on the brass beak, lifted it and let it fall. Once would not be enough. Tap! Tap! Tap! The droning ceased and the house was quiet; its occupants frozen into silence.

The danger of Eliot's situation grew in Sam's mind, until he began to feel a kind of desperation. He knocked again, incessantly this time. He would not give up, he vowed, until the door was opened. At last he heard footsteps on the tiled hall. Sam dropped the knocker one last time and leaped back. Now he would have to face the woman and keep her talking while Eliot escaped.

The door opened, just a crack. 'What d'you want?' asked Freya Greymark.

'Collection,' said Sam, 'for – er – Famine Relief.'

'Whose famine?'

The unexpected question threw Sam off balance, but only for a moment. 'Africa,' he said.

'Where's your ID?'

Sam's mouth fell open. 'ID?'

'Identification,' she snapped. 'I'm not a fool. I'm not likely to hand money over to any Tom, Dick or Harry, am I?'

'Um . . .' Sam fumbled in his pockets. Now would be the time for Eliot to run. He pulled out a library card. Then he heard the banging. It came from a door close behind the woman. Sam scowled at Miss Greymark and said, 'My friend's in there. Let him out.'

She gave him the sort of look that could turn a boy to stone, but Sam's foot was in the door before she had time to slam it. 'Get out!' she hissed.

'No!' His legs were trembling but they held their ground. 'If you don't let my friend out I'll shout the house down.'

'Huff and puff away,' she snarled. 'I'll call the police.'

'Go on, then,' he dared her, 'kidnapper!'

To his astonishment she backed away down the hall. With her eyes still on him she turned the key in a door beside her and Eliot erupted into the passage. He tore past Sam and bounded into the street. Sam followed.

They raced along Salter Row and didn't stop until they reached Fly Street. Once there, Eliot bent double, holding his aching side, his breath drawn through his lungs in great heaving sighs. Sam leaned against the wall, panting noisily.

'Thanks,' Eliot wheezed as he came up for air. 'How did you know I was in there?'

'Guessed,' Sam replied. 'I can see her door from my bedroom window and I thought it was weird how she was peering into her own house. She must have seen your T-shirt through the net curtains. I should have come sooner but I wasn't sure. Then I remembered what you said about paying her house a visit, not her, but her house, and I just got this feeling that something was wrong.'

'You bet it was. She's a crazy woman.'

'They could get her for kidnapping.'

'I was trespassing, wasn't I?'

'I s'pose,' Sam conceded. 'Still, I don't think she should be . . . on the loose.'

Eliot laughed. 'Come and meet the Pipers,' he said.

'All right.' Sam was pleased to be invited.

Eliot took Sam straight into the kitchen where the Pipers were still sitting round the table. 'Meet my saviour,' he said. 'Freya Greymark just trapped me in her lair.'

'Eliot, what d'you mean?' said Sophie, springing up.

'It's OK, Sophie. It's all over.' Relief was like fresh air to someone who'd been almost buried alive. Eliot felt quite light-headed.

'What happened?' Noni asked.

'It's a long story,' Eliot looked at Sam. 'This is Sam.'

'Samuel Dove,' said Sam.

'What a lovely name,' Violet remarked.

Sam pulled a face.

'And why is Samuel Dove your saviour?' asked the dentist.

Eliot didn't have time to answer him, the girls were into their swing.

'The name of a pioneer, or a Victorian explorer,' suggested Noni.

'No, a Pilgrim Father,' Violet said.

'Can I have something to eat?' Eliot was suddenly aware of his enormous hunger.

'And what about Samuel?' asked Sophie

'No thanks, I've got to go.' Sam began to look anxious. He wouldn't stay, he said, because he wasn't sure his mother knew he'd left the house, and if he was late home he ran the risk of losing precious time at the weekend.

Eliot saw him out. 'So I'll see you, sometime?' Eliot said hopefully.

'Sure.' Sam ran into the darkness that had gathered in the street.

Sophie looked pleased. 'Eliot's new friend looks just right,' she said, smiling at her daughters, who didn't smile back. Had their mother forgotten Freya Greymark?

'Right for what?' asked Eliot.

'For you,' said Sophie.

'Tell us what happened?' Noni begged. 'I can't bear the suspense.'

So Eliot poured out his story, holding nothing back. He built his catalogue of strange events into a frightening tale, accompanied by sound effects of creaks, sighs and whispers, the way his mother used to read him fairytales but, unlike Lily, Eliot would let no one interrupt or question him until he'd reached the climax: the moment he found himself locked in. And the Piper family listened, anxious but attentive, and rather impressed by their accomplished storyteller.

'She locked you in!' exclaimed Sophie in a shocked voice. 'I can't believe it. Something should be done.'

'He was trespassing,' the dentist pointed out.

'Yes, but . . .'

'Go on . . .' begged Noni.

'That's all, really,' Eliot told them. 'Sam came and said he'd shout the house down if she didn't let me out. And so she did. And we just ran like hell.'

'I don't like it,' Sophie murmured. 'Something's wrong with that woman.'

'Eliot, I don't think you should go anywhere near her,' advised the dentist.

'A heady mix . . . you and Freya Greymark,' said Noni.

'A poisoned cocktail,' added Violet.

'But you were very wrong, Eliot.' Sophie had to say it. 'I can't think what possessed you. Sneaking in like that. It's just not done – over here.'

'Why did you do it?' the dentist asked more kindly. 'Are you going to tell us?'

'Can't you guess?' said Eliot, and whispering into the circle of bemused faces, he told them. 'For the ring. I did it for Mary-Ellen.' When an anxious silence greeted this remark, he added, 'She won't stop, you see, until she's got it back.'

'Oh, Eliot,' said Sophie sadly.

He realised then that it had all been for nothing. They had listened to his story and believed every word. They could accept that Freya would burn flowers as some sort of terrible revenge. They could be entertained by an account of the Rinaldi family, and did not doubt that Oliver had stolen Orlando's ring. Yet, when it came to Mary-Ellen's ghost, he knew that he had lost them.

'I'm tired,' Eliot said and walked out while they were throwing anxious and embarrassed looks at one another.

Upstairs he found some airmail paper and began a letter to his grandparents. It was several weeks since he had written and he owed them two letters. They already knew about the house in Fly Street, the Piper family and the town, but there was one thing that he had never told them. Now he asked,

Can you tell me, are there ghosts? Have you seen one, ever? Because I have and no one will believe me. And if there are ghosts, why do they choose only some people to visit. If you are haunted does it mean that you're wicked? I know now that my dad has seen the same

ghost, but he never told me about it. Sometimes, I think he wants to cut out every little thing that ever happened to him before Mum died. But I guess I'm still in his life whether he likes it or not. Most likely not.

He described his visit to Dove Farm; the shining grass, the cloud of birds, the new black bicycle and the farmyard that he recognised and yet had never seen. He told them the history of Mary-Ellen and Orlando, Freya and Oliver and the Rinaldi ring, and he found himself ending with words that popped into his head and scared him, just as they would scare the two who read the letter.

Soon I will have to do something that might shock you when you hear of it. I hope you'll forgive me because it's something I really can't avoid. Have they caught those boys? You know the ones I mean. I wish and wish and wish that it had never happened, that I'd killed them first.
Love from
Eliot
Please write back soon and tell me about ghosts.

After he had taken the letter to the post next day, he wandered into the town and there, on a bench that encircled a flowering cherry tree, he saw two familiar figures. They were sitting close together and gazing up at the canopy of blossoms.

'Hi, Mr Bean, Mrs Bean!' called Eliot.

They smiled delightedly, shuffled even closer and Mrs Bean patted the bench beside her.

'How come you're in Saintbury?' asked Eliot, sitting down.

'Fred had to see the dentist again, your cousin, so I thought I'd come in too, and browse about.'

'Have to get going in a minute,' Fred rubbed his jaw. 'You can keep Mrs Bean company while I'm under the knife.' He winked at Eliot.

'Sure.' Perhaps he could persuade Mrs Bean to tell the secret she had been witholding.

Mr Bean looked at his watch and stood up. 'I'll be off now.' He touched his wife's shoulder and she watched him walk away.

'He'll be all right with Mr Piper,' Eliot assured her.

'Of course he will,' Mrs Bean took his hand. 'It's just that Fred's a bit of a baby when it comes to his teeth. He's afraid of losing the lot.'

Eliot grimaced sympathetically. 'Mr Bean's teeth look fine to me.'

She nodded. 'Shall we take a little walk then, Eliot? Or do you want to run on? I expect you've got important things to do.'

'No I haven't, Mrs Bean.' Eliot decided to plunge straight in. 'Matter of fact I wanted to ask you a few questions.'

'I thought so,' she said.

'How did you know?'

'There's something about you, Eliot. I'm not good at explaining these things, but a little scrap of the past seems to have crept up and lodged itself in you.' She laughed. 'There, I don't know what I'm saying.'

Eliot knew. 'It has something to do with Mary-Ellen, hasn't it?' He hesitated, seeing her frown, then ploughed on. 'I've seen her, Mrs Bean, in my room, the room she was locked up in. It's her that's lodged in me. Sometimes, when I look at things, it's like *she's* seeing them through me. She gets angry, but the Pipers think it's me, and the funny thing is, they're right, because I am angry.' He glanced at Mrs Bean again. She was taking him very seriously, but her small face with its crosshatch of wrinkles was still hiding a secret.

Eliot told her everything that had happened the previous day. But although old Mrs Bean looked shocked and intrigued at times, she would give him no explanation. When he mentioned Samuel Dove, however, she smiled with relief.

'Samuel Dove,' she exclaimed. 'Well I never. It's a small world. He's related to Fred and to old Nancy. Now there's someone you ought to see. She could tell you about Mary-Ellen.'

'I tried to see her,' said Eliot. 'But she's very ill. Her carer wouldn't let us in.'

'Oh my goodness.' Mrs Bean stood up. 'Poor old Nancy. I must go and see her. Wouldn't let you in? Oh, dear. She's over ninety, you know. Dear! dear! dear!'

Eliot wished she would sit down again. He wanted to ask more questions. He touched her sleeve, 'Please, Mrs Bean, would you tell me just one thing? Did Mary-

Ellen ever come to Dove Farm? Mr Bean said he saw her there.'

She sank down, heavily, and sighed. 'Yes. She brought her young man over, a great many times, so Fred's mother told me. They liked to go walking. And she came again . . . and stayed . . . for a while, after . . . he was killed, so I believe.' She gave him a sudden quick stare, then, almost afraid of what she had seen, she shook her head.

'She got better then?' said Eliot. 'Or they wouldn't have let her out, would they?'

'I suppose not.' Mrs Bean spoke cagily, and then smiled as her husband appeared and walked up to them.

'It's all over, Elsie,' he said, patting his jaw. 'Good as new!'

Mrs Bean sprang up and took his arm. 'Eliot says Nancy's bad,' she told him. 'I want to get her some flowers,' she tugged him, impatient to get going.

'Goodbye then, Eliot.' Mr Bean winked. 'Women, they're always in a rush, aren't they?'

'I have to get back, too,' Eliot said. He had hoped to talk about his mother, he realised. It would have been so much easier to talk to someone who didn't know his history. But Mrs Bean seemed anxious to escape him. So Eliot murmured, 'Goodbye,' trying to hide his disappointment.

'Goodbye, Eliot,' she said. 'We'll meet again, soon!'

They walked away, leaving Eliot feeling cold and undignified. Why had Mrs Bean rejected him so suddenly. As he walked back to Fly Street he tried to recall every sentence of their conversation. It had happened at the very end, with that quick fearful look at him. What had she seen?'

He began to run, his feet acquiring a speed he hadn't chosen. Avoiding Salter Row he took a route through the town and found himself lost in a maze of narrow cobbled streets. There was a dank feel to the air and a musty, unfamiliar smell. Somehow, the sounds were different. The continual roar of traffic had been exchanged for something older and more mechanical. All around him there were quick footsteps of people he couldn't see. A horse and cart jolted behind him, yet there were no horses to be seen. And now the sweet, floral scent washed over him and he knew *she* was near, her footsteps neat and small. When he lengthened his stride she tiptoed swiftly over the cobbles, anxious to keep pace.

Eliot ran faster, towards the real traffic that sped past the end of the alley. He burst out on to the pavement that bordered the main road and into the monotonous buzz of the present. Keeping his eye on the life of the city, afraid that it might disappear again, he ran towards Fly Street. But this time the real world stayed with him; everyday, recognisable objects swinging round him: lampposts, shop windows, people in jeans and short, bright jackets.

He took one long look down Fly Street and then slipped into the Pipers' house. The place was quiet and empty, and Eliot dashed up to his room. But *she* had reached the room before him and she was angry. It was a deep, smouldering emotion that plucked and pushed him round the furniture, lifting clothes and books in a frenzy, opening drawers and rattling cupboards. He found he was searching for something. *Orlando Furioso*. Of course, they'd kept it away from him after the accident.

Eliot opened a drawer, felt inside and touched the sliver of glass. He took it to the window and sunlight turned it into a blazing spear. It lay across Eliot's palm, four inches of glass, razor-sharp. Perhaps with this he could have saved Lily. But what should he do with it now?

August 1917

From her window Mary-Ellen watches her mother cross the road, a basket over her arm. She wears a dark cotton suit, and Mary-Ellen notes the shorter skirt. Mrs Flowers has gone to join the bread queue. Mary-Ellen can see the end of the queue reaching right round from the Home & Colonial in Vincent Street. She doesn't want the bread her mother gives her, and still drops it, crumb by crumb to the sparrows on the pavement. But her parents insist on giving it to her. Before Mrs Flowers left the house, she slipped a leaflet under Mary-Ellen's door. It's useless to Mary-Ellen. What would her mother have hoped to achieve? For it read:

> *I am the wasted slice of bread, the bit left over. If you collected me and my companions for a whole week, you would find that we amounted to 9,380 tons of good*

bread. Almost as much as twenty German submarines
could sink. When you throw me away you are adding
twenty submarines to the German Navy.

'A silly, silly message,' ranted Mary-Ellen. 'Why should I care? For me the war is over. Over! Over! Over!'

Now her father is leaving the house. His shoulders sag over his hollow chest; an asthmatic, he didn't have to go to war like Orlando, like Oliviero, and Bertie Dove. His shoes are polished, his coat well-pressed, his bowler brushed. A tidy man, now the manager of the bank. Mary-Ellen is a disappointment to him, an embarrassment.

In the hall below, Ada is washing the chequered floor tiles. Mary-Ellen can hear the clank of the bucket, and water dripping from the floor cloth. She bangs on the door. 'Ada! Ada! Bring me my book. My *Orlando*!'

'I can't, Miss,' Ada shouts back. 'They said you weren't to have it.'

So the punishment continues. But the book Orlando gave her is all she has left of him.

'Ada! Can I have some water. It's so hot today. I'm dying of thirst.'

'I daren't, Miss. They said I weren't to open your door till they were back.'

'Curse them!' Mary-Ellen paces her room like a furious cat. She bangs on cupboard doors, snatches at drawers, slides them open and throws her clothing on to the floor. At last she finds it: the small spear of glass from her broken mirror. How providential. With this she can retrieve her precious book. 'Ada, please!' Her pleading is wistful and sweet.

Ada rings out her cloth and trudges into the kitchen. Now she is climbing the stairs; she's a heavy girl and grunts with every few steps. At last the door opens.

Mary-Ellen grabs Ada's empty hand and holds the spear of glass over her wrist. 'The book!' she says.

Ada's reaction is not what she expected. The girl's eyes hold a sort of fear, but the lids are raw and red, her heavy features show a pained acceptance. 'Can I put the jug down, Miss?'

Mary-Ellen drags her into the room and Ada plants the jug on the small table by the bed. 'Now, the book,' Mary-Ellen demands. She holds the glass flat against Ada's skin. If the girl moves, the artery will be cut.

'I might as well be dead.' Ada speaks wearily. Her eyes are glazed, misty-looking.

Mary-Ellen relaxes her grip, her voice is unsteady. 'I don't want to hurt you, Ada. I just want the book. I've nothing else.'

Ada's mouth trembles and tears suddenly spill down her cheeks. 'I do understand, Miss,' she sobs. 'My Huwie's gone, see. My fiancé. Mum gave me the news last night. I'll never see him again. He was swallowed by mud, drowned, Miss, near a place called Wipers. Slipped off the duckboards and drowned.' A terrible wail breaks out of Ada.

Mary-Ellen doesn't hear the front door close or her father's footsteps in the hall. She enfolds the girl and they cling to each other, both sobbing now. Ada lays her head on Mary-Ellen's narrow shoulder, and says, through choking sobs, 'I know you're not mad, but you've got to make your dad believe it. They're going to send you away. I heard them talking about it. They'll chop off all your lovely hair, and lock you up in some awful dark place with really crazy people. And you'll never, never get out.'

'But, Ada, I've got you. Why should I be sent away?'

'They need more girls in the munitions factories. I've got to start next week. Oh, Miss I dread it.' She chokes on a sob. 'I like living here . . . even when you're bad.'

'Ada,' Mary-Ellen hugs her tight. 'I'm sorry I've been cruel. I'll miss you so much.'

'You mustn't act mad any more,' Ada says gravely. 'Make them believe you're well, Miss. I couldn't stand to think of you in one of them loony bins.'

A voice says, 'Ada, get away from her.' Mr Flowers stands in the open doorway, his long face ashen.

'Poor Ada's fiancé has died,' says Mary-Ellen. 'I was only comforting her.' She takes a step towards her father.

'Stay where you are!' he shouts. 'Ada, come over here this minute.'

'I'm not mad. I won't hurt her,' says Mary-Ellen softly. 'I'm better, Father.'

'I think not.' He is staring at her hand and when she looks down, she sees blood pouring through her fingers. She's been clutching the spear of glass so tightly that it has sliced deep into her palm. There are splashes of crimson on her blouse and all over Ada's clean white apron. Yet Mary-Ellen had felt nothing.

'I'm afraid you will never be well, Mary-Ellen,' her father says sorrowfully.

His tone is so chilling Mary-Ellen begins to tremble. She is suddenly aware of the terrible pain in her hand.

'It hurts,' she whispers.

11

The moon and the myrtle tree

'Eliot! What have you done?' Sophie moved quickly towards him and grabbed his hand. The glass spear fell to the floor.

'I just picked it up,' his voice shook. 'I must have missed it when I was sweeping the floor. It's so sharp, I only had to touch it.' Blood covered his fingers.

'Come with me.' Sophie took his good hand and led him down to the bathroom where she bathed his hand and examined it closely. 'There's no glass in it and it's not deep enough for stitches.'

He looked away while she covered his fingers in strips of plaster.

'It was such a large piece of glass,' she said. 'How could we have missed it?'

'It was behind the chest-of-drawers,' he lied. 'Must've slipped down when the mirror was . . . smashed.'

She looked at him, suspiciously. 'Come and have some coffee with me and we'll talk.'

'Can I have the book back!'

Sophie frowned. 'That Victorian thing?'

'The one that – injured Violet.'

'It's a valuable book, Eliot. It shouldn't be thrown around.'

'I know.' He gazed at her steadily. 'But I didn't do it, Sophie. I'm not going to talk about *her* any more because you don't like it. I just have to make you believe that I'm OK, that . . .' The sentences that spun in his head were never delivered. He wanted to say that his mother had nothing to do with flying books and shattered mirrors, but Sophie's concerned expression seemed to dam his words.

'I know you're OK, Eliot,' she said. 'Come on, let's have that coffee.'

They went down to the kitchen where she took *Orlando Furioso* from a cupboard and put it into his hands. Eliot sat at the table poring over the rich illustrations; some were in colour, like Pre-Raphaelite paintings. He especially liked the picture of the English Knight, Astolfo, on a winged horse, the hippogriff, flying to the moon where he was to recover poor Orlando Furioso's lost wits. A small line drawing depicted Astolfo being turned into a myrtle tree.

'When was this story written?' Eliot asked. 'It says that it's a modern version of the original poem.'

Sophie told him to look inside the flyleaf, and he found that the poem was first published in 1516. It's author was Ludovico Ariosto. 'Wow!' Eliot whistled. 'It must be older than Shakespeare.'

'And is it good?' asked Sophie.

'It's kind of hard to read,' he told her. 'But, yeah, I like it. The pictures are great.'

'I noticed you'd brought *The Arabian Nights*.

'And *The Odyssey*. Lily read them to me when I was – oh, long ago.' He'd spoken his mother's name at last.

The telephone rang and Sophie flew to her office. Eliot carried *Orlando Furioso* away.

He spent an hour with the book, sharing Orlando's madness, flying to the moon with Astolfo and riding with the Emperor Charlemagne. Then he took up the other books, *The Arabian Nights* and *The Odyssey*, and, holding each one in turn, let the pages slip under his fingers, while his mother's distant voice told the stories.

When the girls came home, it was all too obvious that summer exams had begun. Not that Violet made much of it, it was Noni who scowled and slammed her way through the house.

'How've you managed to avoid all this agony?' she demanded of Eliot, glaring at him over the tea table.

Eliot, caught offguard, said, 'I guess I was a bit ahead. They thought it wouldn't hurt for me to miss a few weeks.'

'Compassionate leave. Is that it?'

There was an awkward silence before Sophie said, 'Noni, love, there's no need to get so worked up. We know you'll do your best.'

'Yes, but it won't be good enough, will it? It'll never be as good as hers,' and she threw a look of pure hatred at Violet, before storming out.

Violet's head was bent and so she didn't see her sister's

furious glance, but she must have felt it. Eliot glimpsed a tear on the half-hidden cheek, before Violet quickly brushed it away. So much was explained in those few seconds, Eliot could only sit and stare at the table, recalling Noni's past behaviour, and acutely aware of Violet's quiet distress. She sailed through her work like a bird on the wing, knowing everything, yet she could never enjoy her success. Because of Noni, she could only endure it.

'Well,' sighed Sophie, shrugging like a hen with ruffled feathers. 'I'm sorry about that, Eliot.'

Eliot couldn't even remember Noni's words. He was too interested in the sisters' private battle.

'Exams get her down,' the dentist explained. 'Some people sail through; others, like Noni, go to pieces. I was just the same.'

I bet you weren't, thought Eliot. Exams didn't bother him either. He could never take them seriously, but then he didn't have a younger brother as calm and clever as Violet.

Sophie waited until her younger daughter had left the room before confiding in Eliot. 'It's hard for both of them,' she said. 'They're in the same class, you see, and Violet's always been so, well, too bright for her own good really.'

'Noni's not stupid,' the dentist said.

'Of course not,' Sophie exclaimed, 'but she never does as well as . . .'

'Must be tough,' Eliot remarked.

'You see, for all her cleverness, Violet looks up to Noni,' Sophie explained. 'She admires her, longs for her approval, for just one word of praise.'

'And Noni is the only person in the world who will never give it to her.' The dentist's half-moon spectacles had slipped to the end of his nose. His grey eyes smiled over them. 'Don't let all this get you down, Eliot. Those girls'll be different creatures once the exams are over.'

'Can I go to Dove Farm?' Eliot found himself changing the subject. He remembered his half-finished conversation with Mrs Bean, and had a sudden and urgent need to continue it.

'Alone?' Sophie looked concerned. 'It's a long way, Eliot.'

'Please, I know the way. I'll be fine. The Beans asked me. And there's nothing else to do. What's the bike for, after all?'

The dentist and his wife exchanged glances. 'Will you ring us when you get there?' Sophie asked. 'They do have a phone, I presume?'

'Sure. I'll ring from the village if they don't. Promise!' Eliot said solemnly. 'And you have my permission to call out the entire police force if I don't make contact by . . . three o'clock?'

'Two!' said Sophie.

'It's a deal.'

Next morning, Eliot was up and away while the girls were still yawning in bed. With a packet of sandwiches and a can of Coke tucked into his backpack, he rode out of the morning traffic and plunged into the foamy lanes of hawthorn and wild flowers. Late bluebells were still showing, and he passed through woods that seemed to float in oceans of rippling blue. Had *they* come this way? Orlando and Mary-Ellen?

He was still five miles from Hallowater when the sun was suddenly obscured by heavy, purple-coloured clouds. The landscape cowered, ready for a downpour. When it came, Eliot was hurtling through a treeless square mile of crops. The rain caught him full in the face; in a few seconds his clothes were so wet they couldn't absorb another drop, and water coursed off his moving body in flying sheets of silver.

Eliot began to laugh, relishing the violence of the weather. When he reached a bluebell wood, he jumped off the bike and squeezed out his soggy T-shirt. He could hear laughter in the exuberant rush of water that came through the trees, and sang in tiny rivulets under his feet. Orlando and Mary-Ellen. He could see where *they* had sheltered beneath the broadest tree, an oak with a lightning-shattered bough, whose long fingers trailed in the grass.

And when the downpour swung away and he emerged from the wood, it was *their* rainbow that he saw, pinned against a violet sky, and *their* footprints that he followed through the glittering grass. It seemed as though they had left the wood only seconds ago, and that if he ran fast enough he might actually catch up with them.

He leaped on to his sodden bicycle seat and pedalled furiously across the empty landscape. Sometimes, he seemed to see two cyclists drifting ahead of him, one in army khaki, the other in pale dove-grey with a straw hat perched on a dark cloud of hair.

By the time he had passed through Hallowater, the rain had settled into a whispy drizzle, and when he turned into the farmyard it had become a place of shadows, dim and forlorn. The doves had gone and the old buildings sagged under the clouds, their roofs dripping forlornly.

But Mrs Bean looked much the same. 'Well, well. It's Eliot, or a drowned rat. Come in! Come in!'

The stove glowed behind its iron grill and a boiling kettle filled the room with steam. Mr Bean in slippers and a holey cardigan wrenched himself free of an armchair and pulled Eliot close to the stove. 'He's soaking, Elsie. Better dry his clothes.'

'I'll get something warm!' She scampered off to find a dressing-gown and came back carrying a bundle of something soft and brightly striped. She held it up, proudly. 'Fred's new bathrobe,' she said. 'Bought for our holidays. You don't mind, do you, Fred?'

'It'd suit Eliot a damn sight better'n me.' He winked at Eliot.

'Put it on upstairs and bring down your wet clothes,' she told Eliot. 'You can use the little bedroom at the end of the passage. Next to the bathroom.'

The spare bedroom was at the back of the house. Through rain-spattered windowpanes, Eliot looked out over the flattened crops to the distant spire of Hallowater church. When he had wrapped himself in Fred's bright robe, he sat on the bed for a moment feeling a strange rush of blood to his head, not dizziness, but more a sense of unreality, of being spun backwards. Something drew his glance towards the wall behind the bedhead, and there they were: the moon, the hippogriff and the myrtle tree.

Perhaps it had begun as a sampler, one of those pictures children used to make to show off the stitches they had learned, but whoever had made this strange little picture had strayed well away from the usual themes of houses and alphabets.

In the top left-hand corner, a full moon had been embroidered in ivory silk. In the centre, the dark green leaves of the myrtle tree were splashed with star-like flowers, whiter than the moon and so delicately formed it was hard to believe a human hand had made them. Above the myrtle tree, a winged horse rose towards the moon – the hippogriff. There were no cross-stitched numbers on the picture, no alphabet, just a row of random letters running across the bottom. A S T O L F O. Not random at all. For they made a name. But who would guess it? He knew, of course.

Eliot took the picture from its hook and studied the delicate stitches. He ran his hand over the glass, almost expecting to feel the texture of silk. It came close to perfection. Only one tiny stain, at the edge of the moon, marred its flawless shining quality. Was it intentional? Or had someone pricked their finger? And why was the picture here? Eliot took his find downstairs and laid it on the kitchen table.

The two old people regarded it without a word. They

seemed almost to be holding their breaths, and Eliot felt a chill settle into the room. The human silence was so intense it amplified the tick of the kitchen clock and the murmur of the fire. He felt as though he had brought a spell into the room, for the welcoming and cosy place had all at once become mysterious and unexplored.

The moment passed and Mrs Bean, casting a furtive glance at the door, said, 'Let's take those wet clothes, Eliot.'

She seized the bundle under his arm and shook them out. Still not a word about the picture. So it was left to Eliot to say, 'She made this, didn't she? Mary-Ellen?'

'I wouldn't know, dear.' Mrs Bean busied herself hanging damp garments over the clothes-horse.

'But she must have. I know the story, you see. I've got the book, *her* book.'

Mr Bean cleared his throat. 'It's always been here.'

'So she must have been in this house for quite some time, unless she gave it to someone here,' he stopped and added, almost to himself, 'but why would she do that. It's so – personal.'

'Personal? How's that?' Fred asked.

'I'll tell you what it all means,' Eliot offered, 'if you like.'

'You do that, lad,' Fred said, settling back in the armchair. 'Bring the thing up to the stove or you'll catch a chill.'

Eliot perched on the edge of an armchair, afraid that he might never pull himself out of its depths if he let himself slide into it. 'It's about Orlando,' he began. Mrs Bean looked up sharply. 'You see, he lost his wits when his loved one, Anjelica, was unfaithful to him. And

122

somehow his wits ended up on the moon. So his friend, the knight Astolfo, had to fly there to fetch them back. This is the hippogriff.' He pointed to the flying creature. 'Half griffin, half horse. And this is the myrtle tree that Astolfo was turned into by the witch Alcina. I guess you thought A S T O L F O was just a string of letters, didn't you? You wouldn't have known they made a name, an Italian name, although actually Astolfo was an English duke, very handsome, generous and brave.'

'Well, we never knew all that, did we, Fred?' Elsie opened the stove door and poked at the embers.

'I'm not sure,' Fred said uncertainly.

'Why would she put Astolfo, though, and not Orlando?' asked Eliot, willing the two old people to know the answer. 'Did she know someone called Astolfo? Another Italian?'

'You're assuming, Eliot, that Mary-Ellen Flowers made that – sampler, I s'pose it is,' said Mrs Bean. 'It could just as easily have been someone else.'

'No,' said Eliot fiercely.

'The lad's right.' Fred glanced at his wife. 'Mary-Ellen made it. I saw her there,' he nodded at Eliot's chair, 'sitting under the lamp with a white thread in her needle, swinging it this way and that, while she told me stories . . .'

'You can remember her?' breathed Eliot.

'Not clear, like, no. But it wasn't a dream. And when she went, after that terrible day of grief, the house wasn't the same for weeks. I remember that. Everyone felt a dreadful thing had happened. I didn't dream that.'

'What happened, Mr Bean?' Eliot pressed.

'I don't know, lad. They wouldn't tell me. But it was something awful bad. Nancy knows and Elsie's had a stab at guessing. Perhaps you'll get at the truth, Eliot, if you're that keen to find out.'

There was another long silence, filled by the clatter of raindrops on the windowpane. They streamed across the glass like tears and slowly the room began to lose its light.

'Wouldn't think it was June, would you?' Fred remarked.

Mrs Bean took the sampler out of Eliot's hands, saying, 'I tried to get rid of it more than once.'

'Why?' asked Eliot.

'It seemed such a sad thing, not like samplers should be. It's such a hotch-potch, flying horses, an overgrown moon. It doesn't mean anything.'

'But it does,' said Eliot. 'And how come you never managed to give it away?'

'I took it to a jumble sale, but someone slipped it into a box of stuff I'd bought, and when we got home, there it were, under a pile of books.' Mrs Bean was obviously still puzzled. 'So I took it to the junk shop in Saintbury,' she paused and looked at her husband, 'but that were no good either, were it, Fred?'

'It just came back,' he said.

'How?' Eliot wondered, briefly, if the picture had sprouted wings.

'In the post.' Mrs Bean sounded quite resentful.

'So did you phone them, or take it back to the shop and ask how come they sent it to you?'

'No, dear.' Mrs Bean handed the sampler back to Eliot. 'If you must know I were afraid to. It seems that little picture was meant to stay here.'

'Until I found it,' Eliot said quietly.

The old people's eyes fastened themselves on Eliot. A draught rattled under the door and skirted the table. Eliot felt a light touch on his shoulder and knew there were four of them in the room.

February 1918

Mary-Ellen pulls a strand of pearl-white thread to the back of the linen and snips it off. The moon is finished. She has created a mysterious, glowing sphere, a place of secrets. Her work pleases her.

She gazes at the lines she has sketched on to the square of linen. What green should she use for the myrtle leaves? She had only the story to guide her; she has never seen a real myrtle tree.

Needlework has a calming effect. No one hears her screams now, they are locked inside her. She knows she will never again find the perfect happiness she shared with Orlando. But out here in the country she will be all right. Just about.

There are already four generations of Doves in the farmhouse, so it was kind of them to take her in. Beside Mr and Mrs Dove, there's old Granny Dove and Gertie Bean, the Doves' youngest daughter, widowed at twenty-four with a four-year-old boy to bring up alone. The boy, Freddie, has become something of a pet to

Mary-Ellen, following her everywhere and hungry for the stories that she loves to tell.

Sometimes, Mary-Ellen and Freddie walk in the fields, but she is not allowed to go to Hallowater. No one must see her, no one must know. The loyal Doves are sworn to secrecy.

On Sundays a trap brings the Doves' daughter, Lizzie, and her brood to the farm. Lizzie's skin has a worn yellow look though she's hardly thirty. Her blue eyes are dull and she moves in an aimless way, her skinny frame has a permanent stoop, as though an invisible burden rests between her shoulderblades. Mary-Ellen knows that Lizzie's life is more terrible than her own, yet she shared Bertie's life for thirteen precious years. She still wears the ring he gave her before he was blown to bits.

Lizzie always brings her daughter, Nancy, with her. Nancy is the sister Mary-Ellen should have had. She listens and understands. She helps Mary-Ellen to survive.

A sound in the yard causes Mary-Ellen to start. She pricks her finger and a tiny bloodstain darkens the edge of the white, silk moon. Outside, a pony and trap clatters over the cobbles. A voice calls out, imperious and familiar. Mary-Ellen's heartbeat quickens.

A moment later, Gertie knocks and looks in. 'There's someone to see you, Mary-Ellen. A Miss Simnel.'

'Freya!' The needlework slips to the floor as Mary-Ellen jerks out of her chair. She pats her hair, smooths her dress. 'Freya,' she repeats in a frightened voice. 'Why?'

'I dunno. Shall I tell her to go away?'

'No, I'd better see her.' She cannot calm herself

and knows her voice will shake.

Freya has been shown into the parlour. It's a cold, sunless room and the fire hasn't been lit. But it's tidy, and private. The window faces a stiff north wind. In the distant orchard, the trees sway helplessly, and the leaden clouds suddenly disgorge a violent torrent of water.

'Good morning, Mary-Ellen.' Freya stands up and stares hard at Mary-Ellen. 'Are you well?'

'Yes,' Mary-Ellen replies quietly.

'I came to give you news and – and something else.' She holds out a small wooden box. 'Your fiancé was very brave, it seems. Too brave, perhaps.'

Mary-Ellen takes the box and opens it revealing a Victoria Cross on its dark ribbon.

'It's Orlando's,' Freya says. 'It *was* Orlando's, I should say. I went to see Oliver last week and he told me to give it to you. All that is left of his brother, I'm afraid.'

Mary-Ellen studies Freya's face. She has pallid, stony features and a mouth that never smiles. Why does Mary-Ellen see deceit buried behind the sour, yellowish eyes? Why does she have the feeling that Freya is speaking in half-truths? 'Thank you,' Mary-Ellen says, closing the box. 'Are you to be married then? You and Oliver?'

'Perhaps.' Freya regards her own left hand. She flexes her fingers and the ring glistens. 'He's a cripple, you know. It'll be difficult.'

'I'm sorry.' Mary-Ellen avoids Freya's penetrating gaze and watches the pattern of raindrops on the windowpane. Freya knows the ring still has the power to hurt.

'I'm glad to see you so much better,' Freya says.

127

Mary-Ellen nods mutely. 'Did Oliver have anything to tell me? Did Orlando mention me at all . . . before . . .'

'No.'

Mrs Dove bustles in with a tray of tea and stays with them, trying to make polite conversation. Mary-Ellen doesn't hear what they're saying. Her head is throbbing and the effort to hold back tears is overwhelming.

When Freya leaves at last, Mary-Ellen follows her to the door. 'I'd be grateful if you didn't . . . tell anyone about me,' she says.

'No fear of that, Mary-Ellen.' Freya touches her hand with cold fingers, and then she is gone.

Mary-Ellen trudges up the stairs. She sees Freya's visit as a terrible darkness, the night that she has been trying to hold back. Such dreams she had, such wild hopes. But now she knows that Orlando will never come back.

In her room she picks up her needlework and begins to trace a name beneath the myrtle tree. She has made a decision, but it is unbearably hard. In truth she never had a choice.

12
The ring

Mrs Bean wrapped the picture in newspaper and handed it to Eliot. 'Perhaps, this time, it won't come back,' she said.

Eliot was already in the yard, his clothes dry and the promised phone call made. 'Are you sure?' he asked. 'Maybe it belongs here and shouldn't leave.'

'No,' she insisted. 'Let's give it one more chance.'

'I'll come again,' said Eliot, 'and give you a progress report.'

'You do that,' said Fred.

Eliot tucked the picture into his backpack and pedalled out of the yard. 'Goodbye and thanks,' he called, still waving as he turned into the lane.

A week of unusual calm followed his visit to Dove Farm. Eliot kept the picture in his room, but for some reason he couldn't bring himself to look at it. Perhaps he was afraid that it would bring trouble to the house. And he was tired of trouble. He needed a few days of peace. At last the temptation to seek someone else's opinion became too great. He took it downstairs when he knew the girls were at home.

Noni was alone in the kitchen. 'What's that?' she

asked as Eliot unwrapped his package on the table. 'You're not going to be one of these junk freaks are you?'

'This,' said Eliot solemnly, 'is the moon, the hippogriff and the myrtle tree. It was Mary-Ellen's. Fred Bean remembers her making it. Isn't that amazing?'

Noni edged closer. She looked drained of anger, and her weary eyes were ringed with shadows. She squinted at the picture. 'Is that a name at the bottom?' she asked. 'Or just letters. It doesn't make sense.'

'Oh, yes it does,' Eliot said, happily explaining, 'Astolfo's a character from *Orlando Furioso*. I'll get the book and show you.'

'Don't bother,' she said. 'I've got revision. Maths. The last exam.'

'I forgot. Sorry. How're things going?'

'Not well.'

'You shouldn't let them get you down,' he said. 'Exams, I mean. Be more positive.'

'And how am I supposed to do that?' she said, adding in an undertone, 'Oh, wise one!'

Eliot made no response to this. He flushed and kept his eyes on the picture.

'I'm sorry,' Noni murmured. 'It's just that I'm in a kind of hell. No, that's too dramatic. Go on, tell me about As . . . what is it? Astolfo?'

Eliot gave her a quick glance, to make sure he had her full attention. 'It's like I said. Astolfo was another character. An English duke. He got turned into a myrtle tree,' he pointed at the embroidered tree. 'You'd think

Mary-Ellen would write Orlando's name, not his. The whole thing's a puzzle.'

'Seems to me there was someone else in Mary-Ellen's life,' said Noni, 'another secret Italian lover.'

Eliot shook his head. 'There has to be some other reason. It looks . . . it feels so – special.'

'Show it to Mum. Maybe she can shed light on the mystery. I'm off to revise.' Noni gathered an armful of books. 'See, I'm smiling, I'm being positive.' She bared her teeth in a rather cheerless grin and trudged out of the kitchen. 'There's an airletter for you,' she called back. 'On the dresser.'

Eliot leaped to the dresser, seizing the scrap of folded blue paper with Morozov scrawled on the back. He clasped the feather-light letter as though it were a treasure and, tucking the picture under his arm, rushed upstairs.

His grandfather's writing was overlarge and spidery, as though he had written with great urgency.

> *My dear Elioshka,*
> *Your letter was so good for us. We worry, your grandma and me, that you are not with your real family. Gilbert should not have sent you away. But there, he is a sad man, your father. Still he grieves. Lily was his life, and you also. But you have found good people, I think. Gilbert was lucky to have such a cousin as Sophie. He was an only son, born of a lonely man . . .*

'Lonely. Only.' Eliot repeated the words. 'Lonely, only. Only, lonely.' They seemed to share the same meaning, describing someone separate, detached from a wholesome family circle. Now that Lily was gone it seemed to apply to him. He read on.

> *Gilbert once told me that your poor grandfather never knew the identity of his natural parents, and was troubled because of this. Perhaps the Latimer people who adopted him were not kind. Though this may not have been the case. Perhaps he had a melancholy temperament and passed this on to Gilbert. You know he died when Gilbert was only fifteen. You say that you and your father saw the same ghost. Then, Elioshka, it seems to me that in some way she is part of your history.*
>
> *Now listen to me, Grandson. Do not frighten us and say you will do something shocking. This is not you, Elioshka. You are a good boy. Write to us again, very soon, and tell us everything. Your grandma needs to hear from you. She is not doing so good. To see you would be even better.*
>
> *Your grandpa,*
> *Dmitri Alexeyvich Morozov*

'Are you part of my unknown history, Mary-Ellen?' Eliot rested his hand on the little picture. Beneath the glass the sphere of ivory silk seemed to move as though invisible fingers were still drawing it through the linen. What had been on her mind when she made these shapes? Why a myrtle tree instead of Astolfo in his human form? Was he a secret, someone connected to that terrible day of grief that occurred while the needlework was still in progress? If only Mr Bean could remember what it was.

There was a tap on his door and before he had time to answer, Noni sidled in, closing the door softly behind her. 'I've had enough,' she whispered. 'Numbers are dancing in my head and making no sense at all. Wherever I look there's a top-heavy fraction or an algebraic riddle.' She moved into the room, her voice gathering strength. 'I daren't go into the kitchen or watch telly. They'll say, "Come on, Noni, another half an hour." Or they'll try and test me or something. I hope you don't mind me chilling out in here for a moment?'

'Course not.' He was flattered that she'd chosen his room for a refuge.

'You're still puzzling over the moon and the myrtle tree.' She sat beside him on the bed.

'Yeah!'

Noni took the picture and studied it. 'The stitches are so neat,' she observed. 'How long can it have taken her?'

Eliot shrugged. 'Mr Bean says when it was finished something terrible happened and Mary-Ellen left Dove Farm for good. She'd been staying there for some time, you see. Well, there was a day of grief so . . . so awesome the house wasn't the same for weeks. He was very little and they wouldn't tell him what the trouble was about. The picture upsets Mrs Bean because it's so odd, but when she tries to give it away, it always comes back to Dove Farm.'

'Not this time, it seems,' Noni remarked.

'Not yet,' he said. 'Maybe there's a kind of message in it, for me.'

'I can't see a ring,' said Noni. 'I thought all Mary-Ellen's messages concerned a ring.'

'Just because we can't see it, doesn't mean it's not there.'

'Has she disguised it, then? I hope she doesn't start throwing this around, like the book.'

'You believe me,' he stated quietly. 'Don't you?' And because her face was grave and her eyes held a caught-out expression, he knew that she had probably always believed in Mary-Ellen, and may even have seen her.

'I believe you,' she said.

'Why didn't you tell them?'

'I couldn't. I was glad to see you in trouble. It was great to know someone else was having problems, being treated like a weirdo.'

'Why?' asked Eliot, astonished and a little frightened by her honesty.

'Because that's what my life was like before you came. Ever since I can remember, Violet has always achieved things before me: reading, writing, tying shoelaces, piano, riding a bike, swimming, maths, every, every damn little thing,' her voice began to rise and Eliot watched in consternation as she swung about his room. 'Even cooking and ironing and . . . and growing things. It's so, so . . . tiring. It wears me down.'

'But you've seen Mary-Ellen,' he said, 'and Violet hasn't.'

'I haven't *seen* her,' she snapped. 'I've just . . . sensed her.' She dropped down beside him again. 'No, it's more than that,' she confessed. 'Things move, sometimes, little things like my hairbrush, books and stuff. And there's a fragrance in my room even in winter, and footsteps, sometimes. And once she sat on the end of my bed, when I was really down and kind of shared my misery.'

'Shared?' Eliot's concentration was intense. 'How, shared?'

She glanced at him and explained, 'I was feeling really sorry for myself one day, and you know how it is when you have to take great gulps of air to stop the sound of crying, and you feel this great weight on your chest, like you're being suffocated? Well, I was lying there, choking on misery, when this sound came from the foot of my bed. It seemed to be my voice and my tears, but someone was crying *for* me, and the sadness was deeper than mine by far.' Noni turned a frowning face to Eliot. 'It was an ocean of grief, so huge my own troubles were just lost in it. I never felt quite so bad again. Angry, yes, and depressed. But I know that there are troubles out there, much worse than mine.'

'Yes,' Eliot said, and at this point he almost mentioned Lily and the bloodstain like a butterfly, but he didn't know how to start down that road. Perhaps he'd lost the way forever. So he said instead, 'You've got a sixth sense, Noni. I guess that's worth more than good marks at school.'

'I can't see how.' She shrugged. 'Some of us are lucky enough to be blessed with both.' She gave him a wide grin to show that she wasn't resentful, then leaped up, flung out her arms and made for the door with long, swaying steps. She had gone while Eliot's reply was still forming itself in his head, and the words, 'I'm not lucky, Noni,' were muttered at the closed door.

He had a premonition that the picture would keep him awake that night. But this didn't stop him from propping it against the wall, just where the mirror had been, so that it seemed to become a mirror itself, reflecting light well after dark. And Eliot, with his eyes half closed and fighting sleep, saw the glowing ivory moon gathering brilliance until it blazed free of the glass and sailed closer and closer. It hung like a giant lantern, above his head, while the myrtle tree sent never-ending branches round the walls, and the hippogriff stirred the air with its burnished feathers. But it was the name, Astolfo, that shone brightest of all, each letter picked out in dazzling strands: ruby, pearl, sapphire, pearl, sapphire, pearl and ruby. The colours of the ring. It was there, after all.

Eliot got up. It was not yet dawn but the sky had a pale, cloudless light, strong enough to see by. He went downstairs and out into the street. Such quietness greeted him, it was as though the whole town had stopped breathing. But he could hear his own footsteps on the paving stones: a soft padding, like a creature after prey.

He turned a corner, increased his pace, began to run. When he reached Freya's door, he had only to turn the handle. The door was unlocked, just as he expected. Softly, he closed it behind him. Now he must wait.

Soon birdsong gathered in the street outside, and a weak light filtered down from a window on the landing. Eliot moved closer to the staircase; he put one foot on the first tread. If necessary he could wait forever.

Freya emerged at last, a depressing sight in her dark robe, lifeless hair framing her grey, neglected face. She wandered to the bathroom without seeing him. On her return she stopped, took a sudden breath and frowned into the hall. 'How did you get in?' she demanded.

'The door was open.' He had the strange sensation of using someone else's voice.

'Nonsense, the door is always locked.'

'It makes no difference.'

Freya's cautious expression became fearful. Was it this new way of speaking that Eliot seemed to have acquired, or the words that came unbidden?

'Go away,' she said hoarsely, and now there was something not-quite-Freya about her. She seemed to be a younger, healthier version of herself.

'I'll go. When I have the ring. I must have it, don't you see? It's mine.'

Freya tightened the belt on her robe and grasped the banister. 'You'll never have the ring,' she said icily. 'You'll never have anything now. Because you're going to be locked up. You're quite demented, my dear. You just don't seem to know it.'

Eliot, stunned by the chilling words, tried to call out anything to explain himself and prevent the terrible prediction, which he found himself believing. Locked up? He couldn't move, couldn't utter a sound.

'Oh yes,' she went on confidently. 'You've gone too far this time.'

'No,' he moaned and, his own voice flooding back, cried, 'Help me!'

His cry was answered by a sudden stirring in the air, sinister because the whirling dust motes took on a mysterious glitter. Outside, the trees untroubled by any breeze were silent, yet in Freya's house a storm was brewing. She looked about, uneasily, trying to guess the source of the sudden draught. She sniffed the air, smelled flowers, and knew. As she covered her face with her hands, a bolt of fury tore through the house, battering doors and windows, snatching at threads and screws, tearing curtains, paper, glass, until the whole place seemed to be filled with radiant energy, a storm of brilliant, burning rage.

The woman at the top of the staircase threw out a hand and the ring was sucked from her finger. A circle of light spun down and fell into his palm as the woman toppled forward. But Freya's heavy tumbling body never made a sound.

13

The hospital

April 1918

Mary-Ellen watches the landscape drift by; an endless spread of green, brilliant with spring rain. The orchards are alight with blossom, the sycamores already in leaf. Only the oaks are naked, dark and wide; beneath them bluebells are beginning to show, like tiny splashes from the sky.

The train plunges into the dark, changing its tune. Another tunnel. Nancy grabs her hand, this is Nancy's first railway excursion and she is continually surprised, excited and terrified.

Mary-Ellen murmurs, 'We're almost there.' She had to bring Nancy. To travel alone on such a mission would have been unbearable, and no one else would accompany her. They tried to prevent her journey. 'Morbid,' her father called it. 'Leave it alone, what good can it do to see Oliver?'

'Freya won't like it,' Mrs Flowers warned. 'Her mother gave me the address on the strict understanding that it was for correspondence only. *Not* a visit.'

'I want to see him, Mother,' Mary-Ellen persisted. 'There may be words that he can only say in secret to me. A message from Orlando, perhaps.'

'Leave it, Mary-Ellen. Orlando's gone. Forget him,' her father turned his back on her.

'*No!*'

'We'll not accompany you on such an ill-advised excursion,' her mother muttered in a bleak voice.

'I'll go alone.'

But she had invited Nancy. She had to have someone's hand to cling to if the visit went badly. She was afraid of what she might find out there, in the place where damaged soldiers spent their days: shell-shocked, ruined by mustard gas, blinded, crippled, mute. But she must go for Orlando's sake.

They walk to the hospital. It is only a mile from the station and the weather is warm and clear, the grass verges brimming with wild flowers.

The hospital is a vast grey-stone building, set in a garden that rolls, in velvet lawns, right down to the road. There are low hedges, neatly clipped and, in the centre of the circular drive, a pond with a fountain. In the distance, groups of giant trees shelter men in wheelchairs. Some of them seem to be staring up at the sky. Closer to the building, there are a few wicker beds on wheels, and the men lying on these are covered in blankets, their faces white and haunted.

Mary-Ellen and Nancy walk close together, their hands entwined, up the path and on to the steps that lead to a set of glass-panelled doors.

'I've come to see Lieutenant Rinaldi,' Mary-Ellen speaks up confidently, 'Oliviero Rinaldi.'

The woman behind the desk looks up. She is stony-faced, dressed in blue with a starched white cap and collar. She studies Mary-Ellen. 'Are you a relative?' she asks.

'No, I'm a friend of his fiancée, Freya Simnel. Freya's not well, so I said I'd visit the Lieutenant and bring him this.' The lies slip out like syrup and she smiles as she proffers the box of cakes. They came from the Rinaldi's very own shop, though there are no Rinaldis there now, and never will be, unless Oliviero takes over.

'Name?' asks the woman brusquely.

'Mary-Ellen Flowers.' Mary-Ellen glances at Nancy who nods reassuringly.

The woman consults a card and asks a passing nurse where Lieutenant Rinaldi can be found.

'The verandah, most likely,' she is told.

'Go through those doors to the end of the corridor. Turn right and take the first door on your left. It's a nice sunny place.' The woman smiles for the first time. 'I can't spare anyone to take you,' she says.

Nancy whispers, 'I'll stay here,' as Mary-Ellen makes for the first set of doors.

The corridor seems endless. Mary-Ellen's feet begin to skim the surface of the polished floor; her footsteps are so light she can hardly hear a sound; she finds that she cannot stop herself from running. She turns a corner, sees the door. Her yearning hand reaches for the handle but its cool surface makes her all at once afraid.

She opens the door and enters a place that is both

141

beautiful and terrible. The verandah is enclosed by glass and the brilliant sky, the grass and flowers seem to flood the narrow space. There is a row of wheelchairs set against the wall, their occupants gazing at a garden they cannot reach. Perhaps they don't believe in it. There were no flowers, no leaves where they have been. The sunlight striking through all that glass is so fierce they cannot hide from it, cannot hide their hollow sleeves or the emptiness beneath the useless blankets.

The faces that turn towards Mary-Ellen show a flicker of interest but no hope. They are young but what they have seen has made them ancient. And then one face shines out of all the rest. It turns away quickly, fearfully. Too late. Mary-Ellen tries to say his name, but there is a vice round her throat. The glass roof begins to spin, the bright lawns swirl and the pitiless light overwhelms her.

Mary-Ellen falls, unconscious, to the ground.

Eliot woke up on the Pipers' front step. The door was locked and he had forgotten his key. But then he was wearing pyjamas and his feet were bare, so he had not intended to leave the house. For a moment, Eliot was amused by his predicament. How had he come to be outside? And then his hand relaxed and the ring he had been clasping fell to the pavement; the Rinaldi ring. Eliot remembered his nightmare. He bent and retrieved the ring; there was no mistaking the tiny pearl in its circle of brilliant gems.

Shivering, Eliot rang the doorbell. There was no movement inside the house. He pressed the bell again, this time leaving his finger on the button for several seconds. Someone thumped down the stairs and crossed the hall. The door opened and Donald Piper blinked out at Eliot.

'Eliot? What on earth's going on?'

Eliot shrugged helplessly and stepped inside.

'Come into the kitchen. You look as if you could do with a hot drink.'

Eliot sat at the table, the ring held tight in his fist.

While the kettle boiled, Donald put tea bags into two mugs. 'Can you tell me what happened?' he asked gently.

Eliot found he couldn't. He clasped the ring so tightly the gems bit into his palm. Deeper and deeper. Would it disappear into his hand? Mine now, said a voice in his head.

Donald pushed a mug of tea over to him. 'Eliot, I think . . .' he sounded wise and careful, 'I think that you've been sleepwalking.'

Eliot nodded. He hoped it was true. He would rather that than the horrible thing he seemed to remember. Perhaps the truth lay somewhere in between. He saw again the heavy, tumbling body and closed his eyes.

They drank their tea in a silence that was not uncomfortable. If anyone had to find him in this state, Eliot was glad it had been the dentist. Sophie and the girls would have made such a fuss.

'Better go and get some proper sleep before the house wakes up, eh?' The dentist grinned. He got up and touched Eliot's shoulder. 'Come on, old chap.'

They went upstairs together and then Donald

watched Eliot climb the last flight to his room.

But Eliot wasn't ready for sleep. He took the ring to the window. In the hesitant, dawn light it looked small and insignificant lying on his palm. But then he took the band between his thumb and forefinger and gazed at the gems as they came alive, their colours glowing and profound. How did it come to be in his hand and why did he feel it belonged to him? He longed to show someone but feared they would take it from him.

He noticed the cold now and got into bed. As he closed his eyes an ambulance sped beneath the window, its siren shattering the stillness. Eliot thought of Freya falling. Had it been a dream? The ring told him that it had not.

He slept deeply and didn't wake until the girls had left for school. Sophie let him help himself to breakfast before joining him in the kitchen. She sat looking into his face for a moment and then, smiling gently, said, 'Donald tells me you've been sleepwalking. Is that true?'

Eliot didn't know how to answer. He shrugged.

'Has it happened before, Eliot? We ought to know in case . . . Well, we should take precautions.'

He shrugged again, grinning weakly.

'It happens,' she told him, 'especially to young people. They grow out of it.' She realised she was having a conversation with herself and said, a little irritably, 'Aren't you speaking today?'

Eliot put down his spoon. He made a great effort to discover what he should be saying, and how to say it, but gave it up and stared miserably at Sophie.

'By the way, something happened in the early hours,' she turned away from Eliot's silent gaze, deciding, temporarily, to evade the problems that it implied. 'Freya Greymark had an accident. She fell downstairs, just like her mother. She managed to crawl to the phone and call an ambulance. Did you hear it? The postman told me. The poor woman's in hospital. I suppose I ought to go and see her. She seems to know so few people.'

Eliot couldn't hide his dismay.

'What is it, Eliot?' The stricken face alarmed her.

Eliot felt for the ring in his pocket. Laying his hand on the table he uncurled his fingers. Sophie looked at the ring.

She knew what it was but had to say, 'What is it?'

Eliot couldn't help her.

'It's Miss Greymark's, isn't it? Eliot, what happened?' She took his hand as his fingers closed over the ring, keeping it safe. 'Please talk to me.'

He couldn't.

Sophie stood up, pressed her fingers to her temples then smiled and said, 'Eliot, I'm going to call your father. I think it's time. This situation can't continue.' She still seemed to be talking to herself. 'He may be in a bad way, but he's being selfish. Always was, when I come to think of it. Self-absorbed.'

She left the room and Eliot heard her dial a number. His father wouldn't be at home, Eliot speculated. He would have left the flat and be driving through the London traffic, his face set, his mobile at his side.

Eliot could hear Sophie's anxious voice speaking his

father's name. The conversation went on for several minutes but Eliot, straining to listen, could only snatch a few words.

'Today . . . I mean it, Gil . . . Yes, it's urgent . . . he's your son.' In other circumstances Eliot would have been ashamed, but now he only felt relief.

'All right, Gil . . . Thanks!' She came back and, giving Eliot a hug, said, 'He'll be here this evening.'

Eliot nodded and returned to his room. He spent the day with *Orlando Furioso* on his lap, dozing and reading. The ring never left his hand. He couldn't rid his mind of Freya Greymark and, after a while, he realised that he must see her. Only she could tell him how he came to be in possession of the ring.

The girls came in at four. The sound of their busy energy drifted round the house, but they never came to his room. Hunger drove him downstairs at last. Noni and Violet flashed quick, too-bright smiles at him, talking both at once.

'Hi, Eliot!' 'What's the news?' 'Your dad's coming.' 'Gilbert, the desirable!'

His father? An odd description, he thought, desirable. Eliot waited for their comments about sleepwalking.

Violet said, 'Don't look like that, Eliot. It's scary.'

He couldn't help how he looked. He turned away from them but, as he stepped into the hall, the doorbell rang. Eliot froze. Sophie said, 'It's probably Gil,' and hastened past him to the door.

A moment later a stranger walked in. Gilbert Latimer's eyes rested briefly on his son, and then he was kissing

Sophie, and the girls were inching closer. Eliot scarcely recognised the man that came towards him. He held out his hand and his father took it for a moment, in both of his. 'Eliot,' he said, 'how are you?' Which seemed a rather inadequate greeting, but then Eliot could find no words at all to welcome his father.

They moved into the kitchen, pulled out chairs, gathered round the long table, set out mugs and plates, put the kettle on. Noni pushed a chocolate cake in front of Gilbert and when he told them he wasn't hungry yet, Sophie said, 'Let us spoil you, Gil. You need feeding up.'

Eliot, standing in the doorway, watched the man who used to be so elegant, and he was shocked. Gilbert looked like someone who'd been buried. His clothes unpressed, his thick hair dull and overlong. His fingernails were cracked and the jutting cheekbones gave his face a haunting emptiness. All that talk of getting on with life, of putting the past behind him, hadn't worked.

'You haven't been eating properly,' Sophie remarked. 'I can tell.'

Eliot thought: if I were there I could cook an egg for him. His father looked so ruined.

It was a dreadful evening. Eliot couldn't seem to find a word to say. If he caught his father's eye he smiled, self-consciously, and quickly looked away.

They sat together on the sofa, Eliot and his father, like people who had only just been introduced, and weren't at all sure if they had anything in common. The girls disappeared to their rooms and Sophie kept the conversation going, what there was of it. Everyone seemed exhausted by the effort of pretending that things were other than they were. But when Eliot said goodnight and left the room, his father followed and, touching his shoulder lightly, said, 'We'll talk tomorrow, Eliot.'

Eliot nodded and ran upstairs, eager to escape the talk before it had begun.

He woke early and, thinking he was up first for once, ran quietly down to the kitchen. But Gilbert had been awake for hours and Sophie, a light sleeper, had crept down to join him. Eliot could hear their voices, quiet and urgent, coming from the kitchen. They hadn't noticed his footsteps and he tiptoed closer, dreading to hear his father's plans, yet desperate to know them.

Sophie had a light, clear voice, but Gilbert's doleful sentences were not so easy to make out. Eliot stood beside the closed door and leaned his head against the wall.

'Why can't you, Gil? You haven't tried. It would be the best thing for both of you.'

Eliot knew what the best thing would be, but his father didn't agree.

'No, Sophie. It doesn't work. I can't . . . we can't relate any more. We remind each other of . . . of the way Lily died. Eliot must bury that scene forever, or he'll never . . . You've got eyes, haven't you? If he went away to school . . .'

'But boarding-school? Gil, you can't. Not now.'

'There'd be continuity.'

'Continuity?' Sophie's tone was scathing.

'He's going, for God's sake,' Gilbert said savagely.

'And the Morozovs?'

'I'm not going back to the States . . . not yet . . . if ever.'

'They're his grandparents. And Eliot's the only part of Lily left to them. What's made you so cruel, Gil?'

Gilbert answered with a moan that was more painful to Eliot than his father's damaged appearance. He would have run back upstairs if Gilbert hadn't suddenly said, 'All this stuff about a ring. What are we going to do, Sophie? Perhaps he stole it. God knows what's going on in his head.'

Eliot pushed the door ajar and slid into the kitchen. They stared at him, anxiously, like trapped conspirators. Eliot walked up to his father and held out his open hand, revealing the ring.

'Is that it?' asked Gilbert coldly.

What had Eliot expected? That the ring would cast a spell? That his father would recognise it and fall into a trance; that all things would be restored to their rightful place, in a land where Lily's heart still beat?

'Did you steal it?' Gilbert's expression was inscrutable.

Eliot's hand dropped to his side and his fingers closed over the ring, protectively.

'Or find it?' His father relented. 'It looks valuable. We should take it to the police.'

Eliot slammed his fist on to the table and the ring rolled out.

'Wait,' said Sophie. 'I've had an idea. I'm going to see Miss Greymark. Shall we take the ring, Eliot?'

He stared at her. At last he would know the truth.

'It's best to get things cleared up before you go home,' Sophie prattled on, but Eliot didn't hear her. He hadn't even entertained the idea of leaving Saintbury. Perhaps he had assumed he would live with the Pipers forever. He picked up the ring and slid it into his pocket.

Sophie rang the hospital and was told they could visit Miss Greymark in the afternoon. 'Why don't you two go for a walk?' Sophie suggested brightly. 'Get out of the house before the girls are down.'

'Good idea,' Gilbert agreed, glancing at his son.

Eliot wolfed a bowl of cereal and followed his father out into the street. They went first to the river, Gilbert's favourite walk. The cygnets skimmed across the water while their parents preened on the far bank. They seemed to bring a long-lost smile to Gilbert's face. 'I remember them so well,' he said. 'The male is a cob and the female a pen. They pair for life you know . . .' He faltered and walked on, but Eliot could have finished the sentence for him: if one dies, sometimes the one that's left can't live.

As they followed the curve of the river, the white foot-bridge came into view and at last Eliot's voice broke free.

'Do you remember the ghost, Dad? Do you remember Mary-Ellen?'

Gilbert stopped in his tracks. 'What?' he said.

'Mary-Ellen,' Eliot said. 'I met these old people, the Beans, and they said, well she said, Mrs Bean that is . . . she said that a long time ago a girl threw herself from that bridge. A girl who lived in the Pipers' house. Her fiancé died in the Great War and she couldn't . . . well, it was like the swans, I guess,' he finished lamely.

'Swans?' His father was staring at him. 'What ghost?'

'They said you must have seen her, Dad,' Eliot said gently, 'because you jumped into the river to save a girl that wasn't there. The odd thing is, they didn't know it was you, my own dad, when they told me. I heard it later, from Sophie. So we've seen the same ghost. There must be a reason, mustn't there?'

'Maybe,' Gilbert allowed. 'I was a bit of an oddball. I've forgotten my teenage years, thank God.' He started striding away from Eliot, anxious to get through the looming shadow of the bridge.

'It means something,' Eliot called after him. 'This is her ring, Dad. I think she gave it to me.'

'That's nonsense.' Gilbert didn't look back.

Eliot followed him. 'Don't send me away, Dad,' his voice, magnified beneath the iron girders of the bridge, plunged after his father, but Gilbert continued to increase the distance between them. Eliot came to a standstill. He waited, under the bridge, until his father was lost in a curtain of thick willows.

Eliot never found him. He returned home alone. When Sophie saw him she asked, anxiously, 'Did you two lose each other?'

'I guess,' said Eliot. 'I don't think he wants to talk.'

'He'll be back soon.'

But Gilbert didn't return for the midday rolls that Sophie had rushed out to buy from the nearest bakery. Sophie and Eliot waited until three o'clock then set out for the hospital.

Sophie wore a frown of irritation. 'Gilbert's lack of consideration is mind-boggling,' she said, flicking the cellophaned flowers she had bought for Freya.

Feeling responsible, Eliot said nothing. His thoughts were already with Freya Greymark. Would she accuse him? Did the events he dreamed of, while walking in his sleep, really happen?

They found Freya at the end of a ward, which was bright with flowers and bustling, sky-blue nurses. Freya looked out of place. She lay propped up on pillows. There were two cards on her bedside table, and a bowl of fruit. Her next-door neighbour had brought them, she explained. She seemed genuinely pleased with the flowers, but she wouldn't look in Eliot's direction. It was as though she were trying to pretend he wasn't there. Sophie would not allow this.

'Eliot has something to show you, Miss Greymark,' she said. 'He found it. No, that's not quite true, we don't know how he came by it. Eliot!' She pulled Eliot closer until he stood against the bed.

The yellow eyes flickered but avoided looking directly into his. Eliot took the Rinaldi ring from his pocket and held it out to her. He might have flourished a lethal weapon the way she recoiled from it.

'Take it away,' Freya breathed.

'But Miss Greymark, I believe it's yours,' said Sophie. 'Please look at it.'

'No,' she muttered and, as she drew back even further from Eliot, her heavy features seemed to lose definition. Eliot, alarmed by the mysterious shift in his vision, tried to bring her back into focus. But still she drifted, further and further, into a rustling shroud of unfamiliar shapes. For a brief moment Freya's lost features reassembled; a strange unhappy woman looked out at Eliot and said, 'The ring's not mine.' Then she was gone.

Eliot glanced at Sophie, hoping for a sign that she had seen the same dreadful shift of shapes, but she seemed quite unaware that anything unusual had occurred. 'Are you sure?' she ploughed on, although Freya had, by now, turned her head and was plucking the sheet up to her neck. 'Should we take it to the police, then? Perhaps . . .'

'No,' came the muffled reply. 'It's his.'

Eliot withdrew his hand. At the back of his mind a small crescendoing voice came to rest. 'Mine,' it said.

Sophie looked perplexed. 'I don't think you understand,' she persisted. 'It must be . . .'

'Keep it!' Freya's head drooped and a strange rasping sound came from her chest. 'The ring's not ours. It never has been. Wickedness is very powerful. If you're weak it can possess you. My weakness was my mother.' She sighed. 'But I'm free now. Please, take the ring and go.'

Sophie gave Eliot a questioning look and said, 'Well, I do hope you feel better soon. I'll come and visit you again, Miss Greymark.'

'I'm leaving Saintbury,' she murmured. 'I'll start again where she can't reach me. There's still a chance.' She turned to them and actually smiled. It changed her face completely.

'Of course,' said Sophie, smiling back at her. 'Goodbye, for now, then.'

Miss Greymark nodded at both of them, and Eliot found he could look into her eyes without feeling frightened.

They retreated quietly from the strange figure with its pale face and its unfamiliar smile, and Eliot whispered, 'She seems almost nice. D'you think she'll stay that way?'

'Who knows, Eliot,' said Sophie. 'The poor woman's obviously not herself. She'll probably come asking for the ring as soon as she's out of hospital.'

'No she won't,' said Eliot solemnly. 'I know it.' He found that he was not surprised by this knowledge. 'I hope Dad's back,' he added. 'When he knows the ring is really mine, and his, maybe he'll talk about Mary-Ellen and . . .' He wanted to add his mother's name but still could not do it.

'Eliot, it's not yours,' Sophie said patiently. 'I can't think why you're so – obsessed by it.'

'Not me, her,' Eliot said, and then quickly he asked, 'Sophie, you're not fed up with me are you? I know I've been kind of troublesome, but I think things'll be OK now.'

Sophie put an arm round his shoulders. 'Of course I'm not fed up with you. We love you, Eliot. I called Gilbert because I thought you needed to see each other. I must admit, I didn't realise your father would be like this. Events have changed him, dreadfully.'

'It sounds like there's no hope,' murmured Eliot.

A thick bank of cloud swept across the sun and they could feel the sudden chill of evening on their faces. Gilbert had not returned when they reached the house. It was after midnight when he rang the Pipers' doorbell.

April 1918

Mary-Ellen is prepared to forgive. She will visit Freya and tell her what she must know already. She can afford to be magnanimous. Overnight the world has changed and she inhabits a place of infinite possibilities. But first things first. The ring. Freya must see that it is hers now, has been all along.

She hums a tune as she trips across the hall, her ribbon tied carelessly, her blouse a little crumpled from yesterday's journey. There's no time for details.

'Are you going out?'

Her mother comes from the kitchen. She has aged ten years in the few months since Ada left. Now there is no one to help with the hardest chores. Mary-Ellen does her best but Mrs Flowers' health has never been good.

'I'm going to see Freya.'

'You're not to upset her with your wild talk.'

'It's not wild, Mother.' Mary-Ellen tries to be patient. 'It's the truth.'

'No . . .'

But Mary-Ellen has gone. She runs lightly down the street. It's such a blustery day, the air's awash with scents. A mirage of the future lures her through the wind, draws her fingers to the falcon on the black door.

Rap! Rap! Rap!

A positive summons but, as yet, there is no malice in Mary-Ellen.

It is Freya herself who answers the door. She reels from Mary-Ellen's incoherent battery of words.

'What are you saying? You're mad.'

'You know I'm not,' pleads Mary-Ellen. 'It's true. I knew in a second. How could I be mistaken? Give me the ring and I'll forget your lies.'

'I've told no lies.' Freya's treachery is hard to watch. 'You shouldn't have gone there. You had no right. It's obvious you're still not well, seeing things that don't exist.'

'You mustn't say that, Freya.'

'I must and I do.'

Mary-Ellen feels her quick temper rise like a flame, but she will not give in to it. She will not let them call her mad. Now she has a core of steel. She will not snap. One day the storm within her will be released, but not yet. 'I only want the ring.' Her voice is quiet and steady.

'Never.'

'Your wickedness will kill you,' Mary-Ellen warns.

The door slams in her face.

Mary-Ellen steps back into the street, blinded by her cloud of hair.

14

The truth

Eliot hadn't thought of Sam Dove for days, yet his cheerful presence was so uplifting Eliot wondered why he hadn't been to see him before.

'Hi!' Sam walked into his room without knocking. 'Auntie Nancy wants to see you.'

'Me?'

'Yes. Soon as you can. Have you had breakfast?'

'Course. It's ten o'clock.' Eliot was slightly indignant.

'OK. Come on, then.'

'I'd better let my dad know.' Eliot and his father had hardly exchanged a word at breakfast.

'I've sorted all that out with Mrs Piper,' Sam told him confidently.

'What's the rush?' Eliot was bewildered by the peremptory summons. 'Why must she see me now?'

'Because I've got a day off school and I can take you there. Come on. Auntie Nancy says she feels good today. Mrs Horner phoned Mum. I'm not sure of the exact words, something like . . . she wants to see the boy from America, the one who says he's related to the soldier . . .'

'But I'm not,' Eliot exclaimed.

'I know.' Sam screwed up his nose and grinned. 'But you were interested, weren't you? I mean you said Mary-Ellen Flowers was haunting you, or something.'

'I guess I did.'

'Come on, then. You'll get on great. She's not like an old person.'

Eliot followed Sam downstairs; as he crossed the hall Sophie called out, 'It's all right, Eliot. I'll tell Gilbert where you've gone.'

'Thanks.'

They slipped out and as soon as Eliot had closed the door behind him, Sam asked, 'Why's your father here, then?'

'I've been in some kind of trouble,' Eliot hedged, and then, as they walked on, he unburdened himself, relaxing in the freedom of just talking. Sam had no trouble in accepting Eliot's extraordinary story, and Eliot told him everything, from the moment he found himself in Freya Greymark's house, awake or asleep, until his visit to the hospital.

'Weird,' Sam agreed. 'I've never sleepwalked.'

'Nor have I till now,' said Eliot. 'You don't think I'm a nutcase, do you?'

'Course not. You've got the ring then, or did you dream it?'

'No.' Eliot took the ring from his pocket.

'It's small, isn't it?' Sam's reaction was disappointing. 'I thought it would be more kind of spectacular. But Auntie Nancy'll be pleased.'

When they reached the house Sam walked in without

knocking. 'She's expecting us,' he explained.

Eliot hesitated. This threshold was suddenly terrifying. Beyond it lay Mary-Ellen's story. The way it happened.

'Don't be scared.' Sam beckoned him in and opened a door to their left. 'Auntie Nancy, this is Eliot,' he said.

And with a few steps Eliot found himself staring at Mary-Ellen's one true friend. She sat in the corner of a sofa with a rug over her knees and sunlit lace curtains behind her. The light made a halo of her white hair and, at first glance, she seemed less than solid, her features a pale blur. But as Eliot drew closer he could see the lines of laughter on her face. He felt himself drawn, irresistibly, towards her smile.

'Eliot.' She patted the empty space on the sofa.

'Hullo.' Eliot sank down beside her.

Sam swung on the door-handle and said, 'I've got to get a few things for Mum. See you in a bit, then.'

'See you,' Eliot said.

Nancy and Eliot smiled at each other while Sam clattered out, slamming the front door behind him. Eliot knew immediately that listening to Nancy Rose would be one of the easiest and best things he had done in a long time.

She began by asking an unexpected question. 'Why did they call you Eliot?' She had a gentle, quiet voice.

'Oh,' he replied. 'I forget.'

'Was it for the poet, d'you think? There was a poet called T.S. Eliot.'

'Yeah, that's it.' He remembered now.

'D'you like his poems?'

'I dunno,' he confessed.

'So, who's the poet in your family?'

He had never considered this question and was surprised by his answer. 'Dad . . . my dad likes poetry. My mum . . .' he hesitated, 'my mum is dead.'

'Eliot, I'm sorry.' She took his hand in her thin, surprisingly warm fingers. 'That's very sad.'

Eliot might have said a few words about Lily. He wanted to. But what words? And how to say them? Besides, his purpose in coming here was to discover the real Mary-Ellen. Every moment with Nancy Rose must be spent in finding the girl who was haunting him. And Nancy knew this.

'So, you're related to Orlando Rinaldi?' she began.

'No, that's a mistake.' Truth between them was essential. 'Sam thought, because I was in the graveyard and kind of . . . interested . . .'

'You look like him,' she said.

'Who?' Eliot was confused.

'Orlando.' Her expression was sincere but anxious.

'Well, that's . . .' Eliot faltered. 'That's a coincidence, but I didn't think . . . I mean I wanted to know about Mary-Ellen and I was told you remembered her, I never thought about your knowing Orlando.'

'But I did know him.' There was an urgency in her voice, as though Eliot should be made aware that knowledge of Orlando was important. 'I remember him very well, in fact. He was the sort of man you never forget.'

'Really?' He looked away from her and said, 'But it's Mary-Ellen who's haunting me.'

She didn't seem at all surprised. 'Ah, well,' she said, 'then we must begin at the beginning.'

'Yes.'

The story came so easily from Nancy she might have been repeating the very same words for days, yet it never once seemed rehearsed. It was rather that those far-off events had always loomed large in Nancy Rose's life. Her first meeting with Mary-Ellen was in 1916 when she'd gone to fetch a bundle of washing from the Flowers' house. Her father, Bertie Dove, had been killed at Gallipoli, the year before.

'My mother was left in quite a pickle with five of us under eleven and another on the way. So she took in washing for a few pence a week. It paid for our shoes and better food for the little ones. But my, those baskets of washing were heavy, and I had to carry them back still damp, all the way from our house in Bentley Street, up the hill to the top of Fly Street, where you live now, of course,' she smiled at Eliot.

'I don't live there,' he said. 'I'm going away soon.'

'Where?' She clutched his hand. 'Where are you going?'

'Back to London, I guess, and then . . . I don't know.'

'Oh, but you must come and see me again, Eliot. You must.'

'I'll try,' he said. 'Could you go on about Mary-Ellen?'

'Ah, Mary-Ellen. Well, one day, when I was staggering a bit under my load, I see this girl flying towards me. She was holding a straw hat on to her head, but her shiny, shiny hair was everywhere. She could never pin that hair down, whatever she did. "You're Nancy, aren't

you?" she said. "You poor thing, let me take that basket."
"No, Miss," I said, but she seized it from me. "You're too little," she said, "and that's our washing you're carrying. It's not fair. You're to call me Mary-Ellen," she said, "and I'm going to fetch the washing from you every Saturday. So you remember." ' Nancy sighed. 'I could have run home when she took the basket from me, but I didn't. I just stepped along beside her, because by then I was under her spell. Already I loved Mary-Ellen more than any living soul.'

'Even your mother?' asked Eliot quietly, trying not to break the spell.

'In a way,' said Nancy. 'Mary-Ellen was the one who listened, who laughed with me and told me secrets. She never failed to lift my spirits. Her smile made people think they were the centre of her world.'

'Are you a poet, by any chance, Mrs Rose?' asked Eliot.

Nancy's laugh was a high, tuneful sound. 'Goodness, no. But if I've read a great deal in my time, then it's all down to Mary-Ellen. She gave or lent me so many precious books, her parents were outraged.'

'I have a book of hers,' Eliot told her. '*Orlando Furioso*. My cousin found it hidden in the floorboards. *He* gave it to her, didn't he?'

'So you found it, after all this time,' Nancy said happily. 'They tried to take it from her, you know, they said it didn't help her . . . disorder. Disorder, my foot. Mary-Ellen was as sane as they were.'

'So why did they lock her up?'

'For a while she wasn't herself, that's true, but who

could blame her? No one understood, you see. No one realised that Orlando Rinaldi was the air she breathed. That's what she said to me before they locked her away. "I can't get my breath, Nancy. Everything seems lost. I can't even feel the things I touch. I think that I am dead; I might as well be." But anyone who had seen them should have known the loss of one would destroy the other. Oh, all lovers think they are exceptional but, Eliot, believe me, Mary-Ellen and Orlando *were* different. Their feelings for each other were so deep, they seemed enchanted. Their joy in each other's company was like a tide, it lapped around you, even complete strangers were swept along, wondering why all at once, they were so happy again. The world was such a dark place. Every day, you see, news would come of some young man's death, someone you knew. How could Mary-Ellen exist without Orlando?'

'But she did – for a while,' said Eliot.

'For a while,' Nancy said wistfully. 'When she was calm, at last, they sent her to Dove Farm, and that's where I saw her again.'

'I found her sampler there,' Eliot exclaimed, 'an embroidered sort of picture. It had the name Astolfo on it, a name from the book Orlando gave her. But I wondered why she didn't put Orlando's name instead.'

'Astolfo was the name she gave her baby.'

For a moment, Eliot was speechless. 'A baby?' he breathed. 'I didn't know she had a baby.'

'No one did. No one except Mary-Ellen's parents and the Doves, and Freya of course, who found her at the farm. It was then that Freya did something terrible. I still find it hard to believe a human being could stoop to such cruelty.'

'What did she do?' Eliot's mouth was dry.

Nancy shook her head and swayed a little. Eliot wondered what he should do if she fell off the sofa or passed out. She appeared to be caught between then and now and wasn't sure how to let the past unfold. At last she found a way. 'Oliver, Freya's fiancé and Orlando's brother, Oliver was in hospital. It was 1918. He'd been badly wounded, but no one knew quite how badly until Freya went to see him. Afterwards she went all the way out to Dove Farm, just to tell Mary-Ellen, and to give her Orlando's medal. A Victoria Cross. In that, at least, she was honest. But the rest was all a pack of lies.'

'What did she say?' he asked.

'She made Orlando's death seem so final. She told Mary-Ellen there was nothing left of him. I think Mary-Ellen had been hoping for a miracle, that, somehow, there was a chance that they could be a family, she and Orlando and the baby. But after Freya's visit she lost hope. They took the baby from her when it was, oh, just a week old – it was a boy. They said it would be cruel to keep the child, an unmarried woman with no means of support. She wasn't allowed to know where the baby went, only that the couple were well-off and childless. But if Mary-Ellen had known the truth, she would never have given up her child.'

'The truth? What truth, Mrs Rose?' Eliot felt a sudden

panic, as though the events of eighty years ago had a bearing on his very existence.

Nancy Rose turned her head away and didn't answer him. And when Eliot peered round into her face he saw that her eyes were closed. He thought there might be tears held tight behind the pale lashes, and he wanted to do or say something that might comfort her. But he couldn't think of anything, so he just held her hand until she felt ready to turn back to him. When she did, she murmured, 'I'm sorry, Eliot. You see it still distresses me. The past seems only one step behind me these days. Soon it'll catch up, won't it?' She smiled.

'Don't talk about it if you feel bad,' he said.

'But you must know, Eliot. I've never told anyone about . . . about what happened. Or at least I was only twelve or thirteen when I did, and everyone dismissed it, just as they dismissed Mary-Ellen's claim.'

'What did she claim?' asked Eliot carefully.

Nancy frowned and stared into the room. Moments passed and Eliot began to think that she had forgotten everything, that their conversation had ended, but all at once she said, 'Why am I telling you this? I've not talked about it for so long, but you want to know the truth, Eliot, don't you, because you've seen her?'

He nodded, saying nothing.

'After the baby was taken,' she said, 'Mary-Ellen had a desperate urge to see Oliver. She wanted to know about Orlando, how he looked, what he said before he died. So she decided to visit the hospital. No one would go with her, they tried to stop her in fact, so she took me for company. While she went to find Oliver I waited for her in this big empty hall. It was so quiet there, and the garden outside, where the wounded soldiers lay, it was unbelievably beautiful. I waited and waited and at last she came back. A nurse was with her. Mary-Ellen looked very pale and she was sort of staring over my shoulder. She'd fainted apparently and I said should we get a cab to take us to the station, but she said no, she needed the air. As soon as we were through the doors she grabbed my arm like she was drowning, and she sobbed – I can hear her now – "Oh, Nancy," she sobbed. "It's Orlando in there. Orlando. I must have blacked out, it was such a shock. When I came round I was in the corridor with these two nurses. I told them a terrible mistake had been made, but they wouldn't believe me." '

'Orlando?' Eliot breathed. 'But I thought – I thought he died in France somewhere, and was never found.'

'That was a lie,' Nancy gave Eliot a surprisingly hard look. 'I don't know who began the lie, but it would have been easy enough. Two brothers, one dead, the other wounded, only days apart. The same name, the same initial, their papers lost, and in all that dreadful turmoil, who would know? Perhaps Orlando let the lie continue for a while, thinking to save Mary-Ellen from tying herself to a cripple. There wasn't much of him left except his beautiful face, that's what she said. As if his being crippled could have changed her heart.'

'But are you sure, Mrs Rose?' Eliot was still wrestling with the story. 'Perhaps Mary-Ellen thought she saw Orlando because she wanted to.'

'As if she wouldn't know,' Nancy said indignantly. 'Of course she saw him. I'm as sure of that as I am that you are sitting there.'

'I'm sorry, I do believe you,' Eliot said quickly. 'But what about his parents. Didn't they know?'

'Mr Rinaldi died of the flu while his sons were still in France. His wife had already passed away. There was no one left but a couple of cousins, and they didn't know the brothers well enough to tell them apart.'

'How did it end, then? Why didn't Mary-Ellen go back for Orlando and bring him home?'

'Because Orlando died before she could. A few days after Mary-Ellen saw him he took an overdose of morphine. Perhaps some kind soul helped him. The pain of lost limbs is terrible, so I'm told. But Mary-Ellen blamed herself. He thought that he'd lost her love, she said, when he saw that his ring was missing from her finger. And that it was horror at the sight of him that made her faint, not shock. The torment almost drove Mary-Ellen mad again, but this time she buried her anguish. Those were the worst months, when Mary-Ellen raged inside, but never let it show. She was chilly and calm, yet somehow deadly.' Nancy nodded to herself and smiled grimly.

The ring might have saved them, Eliot thought. 'Did she jump soon after?' he asked tentatively, 'from the bridge?'

'She didn't jump,' Nancy said fiercely. 'That was another lie. I saw her only moments before it happened. She looked quite reconciled. I asked her if she was going to the peace celebrations. The Peace Treaty was about to

167

be signed at last. She said she'd heard the news but wouldn't be celebrating. She was wearing real flowers in the band of her hat and she looked so pretty. Just before she turned away she said something about her baby, hers and Orlando's; I can't remember what it was . . .' To forget such precious words obviously distressed Nancy Rose, but then she said brightly, 'Mary-Ellen did not throw herself from that bridge, whatever they say. I know. Maybe she slipped. Maybe her thoughts were so far away she was careless. Who knows what she was thinking. Don't believe the stories, Eliot. Not a word. They've always got it wrong. Everything.'

For all her ninety-three years, Nancy Rose had a surprisingly firm grip. Eliot's fingers seemed to lose all feeling as her hand tightened over his, and her blue eyes were so demanding he couldn't look away. Eyes that had seen Mary-Ellen. And Orlando. What did they see in him?

'What does it mean, Mrs Rose?' he asked. 'Why is all this stuff so important to you and me?'

'I loved her,' Nancy said simply, 'but as for you, we'll have to guess.' She smiled. 'Take a wild, wonderful guess and see what you come up with?'

Eliot didn't dare, just then. The door opened and Sam said, 'Hi, you two. I'm starving.'

'Then come right in,' said Nancy Rose, 'and we'll cook something up.'

'I've got to get these things to Mum,' said Sam, swinging a bulging plastic bag.

'And I'd better get going,' Eliot said, standing quickly.

'I'm not sure what's happened with my dad, we're supposed to have a talk about my future.'

'But you'd rather not,' guessed Nancy.

Eliot shrugged. 'No.'

She held out her hand. 'Goodbye, Eliot. Come and see me again soon.'

'OK.' He didn't want to say that this might be impossible. 'Soon as I can.'

How could he have forgotten the ring? He was almost through the door when he thrust his hand in his pocket and touched it. Eliot whirled back and stood before Nancy Rose with the Rinaldi ring in his open palm. 'Look! D'you remember it?'

At last he got the reaction he'd been waiting for. Nancy's eyes became two marvelling circles. She gazed at the ring for several moments, quite speechless. 'How?' she whispered.

'I'm not sure,' Eliot told her. 'That's the biggest mystery of all. I can't explain it. They thought I stole it from Miss Greymark, but I swear I didn't. It just kind of fell into my hand when I was dreaming. She had a kind of accident you see, but the weirdest thing of all is that when I took it to her in the hospital it seemed to frighten her. She told me I could keep it. That it was mine.'

Nancy Rose studied Eliot's face then carefully she folded his fingers over the ring. 'I'm so very glad I met you, Eliot,' she said. 'I haven't felt so happy in years.'

'I'll come back, I promise.' Eliot knew he would keep his word. No one would make him break it.

15
Speaking of Lily

The two boys parted at the Pipers' door and, as Sam ran off, Eliot called, 'I'm leaving Saintbury. I'm not sure when, but soon. I'll come and see you before I go.'

Sam spun round and shouted, 'Just don't go!'

This didn't make things easier for Eliot. 'I'll have to run again,' he muttered as he let himself into the Pipers' hall.

As soon as the front door closed behind him, his father stepped out of the kitchen. 'Where the hell have you been?' he blazed.

'To see an old lady. Sophie said it was OK. She said she'd tell you.' Eliot stared into his father's angry face.

'Sophie's out,' said Gilbert.

'Then she must've forgotten. I'm sorry, Dad, but what's the problem?'

'I wanted you to get packed. We're off soon.'

'Off? Right now?' Eliot was stunned. 'Off where?'

'Where d'you think? I'm not on holiday. We're going back to London. Tomorrow, I've arranged for you to see a school in Wiltshire.'

'Wiltshire. It sounds miles from anywhere.' Panic made Eliot feel sick.

'Well it's not. You'll have a chance to see the place before it closes for the holiday. It's a good school. Loads of activities. You'll have a great time.'

'I don't want to see it,' Eliot shouted. 'You said we'd have a talk.'

'You weren't here,' said his father, 'and I've got things to attend to. I can't wait any longer.' His father turned his back on Eliot and walked into the kitchen.

'Why can't I stay here? What did I do?' cried Eliot, pursuing Gilbert. 'I didn't run away, did I? I didn't do anything awful.'

'You've caused trouble,' Gilbert rounded on his son. 'Sophie hasn't told me everything, but I can read between the lines. You've been violent, cut yourself, seen ghosts, taken a ring that doesn't belong to you . . .' Gilbert paused. 'It isn't fair on them, I realise that now. I'm sorry, Eliot. You can't help it, I know. I think you need to see a specialist.'

'You've seen ghosts, too.'

'Go and get packed,' ordered Gilbert.

Eliot hadn't decided whether to obey when Sophie walked in, cheerfully waving yellow supermarket bags. 'I've bought things for tea,' she said, 'loads of chocolate and wicked creamy things.'

'We're leaving before tea,' Gilbert said quietly.

Sophie didn't seem to comprehend. 'The girls don't get back till four,' she said. 'You'll still be here, then, surely?'

'I don't think so.' Gilbert had the grace to sound ashamed.

'Yes, we will,' cried Eliot. 'I've got to say goodbye to

Noni and Violet – and Donald. I won't go otherwise.'

'Just go and pack,' his father said wearily.

Eliot ran to his room. Furiously, he opened drawers and slammed clothes on to the bed. He pulled his bag from the wardrobe and began to pack. The bag filled quickly. The baseball mitt that Grandpa Morozov had given him took up a lot of space. And the ball was heavy. He should have practised more. To please his grandfather. When could he do that now? And where? When would he see Grandpa Morozov again?

His eye fell on *Orlando Furioso* lying on his pillow. Should he take the book? he wondered. No, because that really would be a theft. What else should he pack? He scanned the room – and found the sampler.

Eliot sat on the bed, resting the picture on his knees. He found himself studying the tiny stitches *she* had made, until he was drawn, like a thread, closer and closer to her. His finger traced the name, followed the curve of the tree and rode with the hippogriff, up to the pearl-white moon. The moon where Astolfo would find a cure for poor Orlando. 'She thought her baby would bring him back,' Eliot murmured. 'But it was too late – it's always too late.'

And now that other picture, the one that he'd buried so well, seeped like spilled water, across the surface of the glass: the shadow of palm leaves on his mother's skirt, her swinging hair with sunlight woven into it, the dangerous little bag, the startling blade-flash and the fatal blood-red butterfly.

Eliot screamed but his voice was swallowed by a

curious thunder. Lost in history. The ever-present drift of flowers became an avalanche. It swept round Eliot's head until he drooped beneath it. He knew what he would see when he looked up.

She was standing by the barred window, threading flowers into the band of a straw hat. Her face was not remotely ghostly, but her eyes were vacant, faraway. When Eliot called to her she looked up. He didn't know what words he had used, perhaps he asked if she could see him. Whatever it was, he had her full attention. She gazed at him, surprised and slightly curious.

'I know what happened,' he said. 'I know why you wanted the ring.'

She allowed a very tiny smile to soften the line of her mouth.

And Eliot found himself saying, 'I think it's time I told you about me – and Lily. Lily was my mother. She had fair hair and blue eyes and she wore shiny silver earrings. She loved stories and me and Dad. She laughed a lot. She was fun. One time, when I was maybe four or five, she bought me this great big silver balloon. It took me right off the ground, right over this little stream in the park, and someone called, "Hey, lady . . . that's dangerous, the kid could drown." And d'you know what Lily said? She said, "My son can fly." '

Mary-Ellen hadn't moved but a kind of light had come into her face.

Eliot continued, 'Last year a boy . . . a boy not much bigger than me . . . a boy robbed me. He had a knife and he tried to rob Lily, but instead he robbed me, and I couldn't stop him.' Eliot's voice broke.

The girl by the window was frowning now and a look of intense pain clouded her dark eyes.

Eliot stood shakily and took a step towards her. 'I have your ring,' he whispered. 'Look!' His hand was trembling and a brilliant spectrum of colour blazed from the ring as it caught the midsummer light. 'But what's the use of it?' he asked. 'How does it help us? And why did you choose me, Mary-Ellen?'

She held his gaze as she came towards him, soundlessly. He couldn't move. She lifted a pale hand and Eliot felt a touch on his fingertips, an imagined breath. She passed him and when she reached the door she put on her hat, pinning it carefully to the mass of dark hair. Then she glanced round the room, and finding Eliot still there, watching her, she smiled. And was gone.

'Where are you going?' he called.

16
The last run

June 1919, Midsummer day

'Where are you going?' Mrs Flowers stands at the foot of the stairs. She looks ill.

'Just for a walk, now that it's stopped raining. I won't be long. D'you want me to fetch something for you?'

'A prescription from the chemist. My chest is bad again.' Mrs Flowers' rattling cough adds emphasis to her request.

'Poor Mum. I'll get it on my way back.'

Mary-Ellen walks down Fly Street. She is smiling, and no one would guess that only last night, when the scent of sweet rocket was at its most potent, she had kneeled in a graveyard with her arms full of flowers. She had pressed her face into the earth and stayed there till dark, so that when she came home no one could see the mud-coloured tears on her face.

Now Mary-Ellen nods as she passes a neighbour. 'Good morning,' she says. 'Yes. Peace at last. It's wonderful.'

At the corner of Fly Street she meets Nancy Dove and gives her a hug. 'I'm going down to the river,' she tells Nancy. 'I feel today as though a weight's been lifted from me.'

'They say there'll be a grand celebration when the Peace Treaty's signed,' Nancy says. 'But Mum says, "What's there for us to celebrate, with Dad blown to bits?" The way I see it though, is that at least my brothers won't have to go to war.'

'You're right, Nancy. But you must forgive us, your mum and your auntie Gertie and me, and poor Ada, all of us who've lost someone . . . we can never celebrate.'

'No,' says Nancy guiltily. 'Course not.'

Mary-Ellen gives a gentle laugh. 'Don't be sad, Nancy. Look at the sky. It's wonderful.' She tilts back her head and a flower slips from her hat-band. She picks it up and gives it to Nancy. 'There, put it in your hair. A flower for peace.' She is about to walk on, but changes her mind and steps closer to Nancy, so that strangers won't hear. 'Nancy, I've been thinking about Orlando's baby. If he needed me, d'you think I'd know?'

Nancy looks anxious. 'I can't tell. Perhaps you would.'

'I hope so.' Mary-Ellen takes Nancy's hand. 'I believe I heard something, you see. The voice was years and years away. But what is time after all . . .?'

Nancy feels the warm pressure of Mary-Ellen's hand, and then her friend slips away. 'I'll see you tomorrow,' she calls. 'I've got some more books for you.' She runs downhill towards the river, her feet tapping over the rain-washed cobbles.

The footbridge is still wet and she slides on the wooden planks. The soles of her shoes are new and too smooth. When she reaches the centre she looks down-river to the old stone bridge that carries the traffic: vans, cabs, horses and carts. And then her gaze is drawn upwards, over the tall trees in the park, north to Hallowater and Dove Farm. She can see the acres of corn and the flight of white birds over the place where they lay, she and Orlando. Where their bodies met and spun. On Midsummer day.

'A dance, Miss Flowers?'

'Signor Orlando, of course.'

'Do you love me, Mary-Ellen?'

'Always and forever!'

'Orlando!' Mary-Ellen leans against the rail and reaches out a hand. Her new shoes cannot keep her safe. Mary-Ellen loses her grip on the world and flies towards the water.

'Eliot, are you OK?' Noni's head appeared round the door.

'I thought you weren't coming back till four.'

'It is four. I was sent to find you.'

Eliot stood up and the sampler slid to the floor.

'Watch out!' Noni leaped in.

But the glass didn't break. He picked it up and laid it on the bed. 'I couldn't fit it in my bag, or my backpack. They're stuffed.'

'We didn't know you'd be going so soon. We thought you'd be here for the summer holidays. That was the whole point, wasn't it?' Noni said angrily. 'I don't like what's happening.'

'Me neither,' he said. 'But I blew it.'

'No, you didn't,' she said fiercely. 'Your dad's got it all wrong.'

He shrugged. 'I've got something to tell you. I know all about Mary-Ellen now. I went to see Mrs Rose.'

'Write to me.'

'OK.'

'Mum's got a great spread downstairs. Your going-away feast.'

'I didn't know it was so late.' He sighed. 'Dad said he wouldn't wait for tea.'

'Well, he did. What've you been doing? He said you'd been up here for hours.'

'I've been thinking about Mum,' Eliot said.

Noni sat on the bed. She looked astonished. 'I thought that you'd never mention her,' she said.

'No one asked me to.' This wasn't quite fair, he realised. 'But I suppose you were all afraid of . . . of what I might do.'

'We were cowards,' Noni confessed. She noticed the book on his pillow. 'Are you taking *Orlando Furioso*?'

'It isn't mine.'

'I think it is now. Violet won't mind.'

Gratefully, he pushed it into his bag. 'All the same, I'll ask her,' he said.

'So what were your thoughts,' Noni asked carefully, 'about your mother?'

'I was just remembering things. The way she looked. How she died. She was beautiful. And I wondered how I could have let them . . .' he looked away, frowning, 'how I could have let them do that to her?'

'Eliot!' Noni sounded shocked. 'You haven't been blaming yourself, have you?'

'I guess I have.'

'You're crazy.' Her arms closed round him and held him tight. He clung to one of her hands. It seemed so much smaller than his own.

'Come on,' she said at last. 'They'll be wondering what we're up to.'

They went down to the waiting feast, and Eliot did justice to all the sandwiches, the cream and chocolate and giant rum babas. There was a feverish atmosphere in the room. The determined smiles didn't fool anyone. Eliot and his father sat with Noni between them, so that Eliot didn't have to think about what would happen when the food had vanished.

But he couldn't stop the clock. After tea they carried the bags out to the car and Eliot asked Violet, 'Can I take *Orlando Furioso*?'

'It's yours,' she said. 'I don't believe in all this, you know. This leaving or whatever it is. You're supposed to live with us now, so where did we go wrong?'

'I went wrong,' he said, and as she shook her head, he added, 'I'll write and tell you everything.'

He almost forgot the sampler and had to rush upstairs and get it.

'What's this?' asked Gilbert. He stood by the open boot as Eliot laid the picture carefully between their bags.

'It's hers, Dad. Mary-Ellen made it herself.'

Gilbert stared at it for a moment and then slammed the boot.

The Pipers had followed them out and now stood in a self-conscious group by the step. The two families kissed and shook hands, and Noni, clinging to Eliot, asked softly, 'What are you going to do with the ring?'

'Guess,' Eliot whispered, close to her ear.

Noni grinned.

Eliot was about to get in the car when the dentist, who'd been unusually silent, suddenly asked, 'In a perfect world, Eliot, what would you choose to do?'

'Stay here,' said Eliot, and then, shocked into the truth, 'I'd live with Dad but come here every holiday.'

'The world isn't perfect,' said Gilbert. He swung into the driving seat and slammed his door. Eliot sat beside him and the car moved off.

They left the Pipers so rapidly Eliot barely had time to wave.

'Come back,' they called. 'Come back soon.'

There was a tailback of motionless traffic on the bridge and Gilbert groaned, 'I knew this would happen if we left it too late.'

The minutes passed as they sat wedged in a sea of exhaust, and suddenly Eliot remembered Sam. 'I've got to see my friend,' he said. 'I promised I would.'

'You'll have to write instead,' said Gilbert.

'And Mrs Rose,' Eliot went on as though his father hadn't spoken. 'And the Beans, I've *got* to see them.' It was all so clear now; how they could be saved, he and his father, if they went to Dove Farm.

The traffic in front began a sluggish advance. Gilbert changed gear and moved after them. But they stopped again in the middle of the bridge and Eliot had a clear view down to the footbridge. 'If you take the next turn left we could be at the farm in maybe twenty minutes,' he said. 'Please, Dad!'

'Eliot, what are you talking about?' Gilbert rested his arms on the wheel.

'Dove Farm, Dad. Where the sampler came from. Where Mary-Ellen's baby was born. If you could see it . . .'

'We've got to get back,' Gilbert said tersely. 'We've an appointment at the school first thing tomorrow. And I want to arrange a summer camp for you.'

'Why?' cried Eliot. 'I don't want to go. I want to stay with you, Dad. I can cook stuff for you. I can look after myself. Lily made sure of that. She wouldn't want me to go away. She'd want me to be with you, Dad. Just come to the farm with me!'

Gilbert rapped his fist on the wheel. Angry. Blocked by the traffic and besieged by his son.

'And in the holidays,' Eliot went on breathlessly, 'I could come back here. Maybe I could go and see Gran and Grandpa Morozov. I won't be any trouble ever again. I know I won't.' And he did know it. 'What am I going to do, Dad? What's going to happen to me?'

'For God's sake, Eliot, not now!' The car jerked foward, down to the end of the bridge where, once again, they were stopped by the traffic lights. To their right a stream of cars lurched towards the motorway. The road ahead ascended steeply to the two churches and the War Memorial. The turn left led, eventually, to Hallowater.

Gilbert didn't hear the soft click as Eliot unlocked his seat belt. The lights blinked to orange and as Gilbert's hand left the brake, Eliot opened his door and leaped out. He did not look back when his father shouted, and Gilbert turned helplessly in the opposite direction, slamming the open door while he manoeuvered past the lights.

As Eliot sped north, the sun threw bolts of heavy light across the road. The sky glowered like a bruise. But the rain held off until he reached the second turn, and then it came in feathery showers that dried at a touch. Twenty miles to Hallowater. He wouldn't need to run all the way, Eliot reasoned. His father would take time to work his way back from the motorway. And then what? How could he explain his rebellious leap into the traffic? He couldn't. But he knew it to be inevitable. Whatever drew him to Hallowater today was as irresistible as the tug of true north on a compass. Will had nothing to do with it. The shower became a downpour and Eliot kept running.

Would Gilbert return for him? He must. Because Dove Farm lay at the heart of what they would become. Some-where in the wide gold fields was a voice, a secret waiting to be heard. And as Eliot ran from his father, so he drew closer. His side began to ache but he couldn't stop. His legs felt lifeless yet he was still in motion. His sodden clothes clung to the heat of his body, and the wet hair clamped to his forehead almost blinded him. He ran like an automaton beamed at a distant light. His burning feet didn't seem to be in contact with the ground. Tarmac hardly mattered, it merely made a passage through the fields.

Maybe I'm flying, he thought. He didn't even glance at the peeling signposts. At every crossroad instinct guided him. Few cars passed and only a farmer on a tractor gave him a cheerful wave. Rain falling endlessly on to the ground seemed to be the only sound.

'I'm always on the run.' Eliot laughed in spite of the pain it caused. 'I'm on the run,' he wheezed, taking a step too near the verge. His toes met the shallow bank and he pitched into the grass.

He opened his eyes on an evening sky as still as glass. Had he been unconscious or sleeping peacefully? He looked at his watch and found it was nine o'clock. How long had he been running? Four hours? Dragging himself from the sodden grass, he looked for a sign. He had known the way, every step of it, until now. But all at once the route was lost to him. And then he saw it, half-obscured by clumps of cow parsley. Hallowater. A few steps further and he could see the hamlet. Behind him an engine purred softly; he turned and saw his father's car, its sleek blue bonnet moving slowly. And Eliot ran.

The car accelerated, and now Eliot was bounding past picket fences, hedges, walls, gates and anxious-looking faces, while in the road the blue car kept just abreast of him.

Gilbert wound down the window. 'Eliot!' he called. 'Stop, please!'

'No!' cried Eliot. 'No! No! No!'

'Please, Eliot. You can go to the farm. Just get in the car.'

Eliot slowed to a walk. 'Come with me, then.'

'I promise.' The car stopped.

They had passed the last house in the village. Now the road climbed steeply. The lane to Dove Farm couldn't yet be seen, but it was there, waiting for them, a secret passage to their past.

Eliot turned and came back to the car. He opened the door and said, 'Can I ask you something, Dad?'

'Of course.' His father's face looked less severe, but very weary.

Eliot got into the seat beside him, and they sat staring ahead, silently, until Eliot said quickly, 'I want to talk about Mum.'

His father seemed to have stopped breathing. 'Yes?' His voice was trapped somewhere, and only an echo of itself.

'We were like a triangle, weren't we? So when one of us got lost, the rest of the triangle didn't make sense.'

Gilbert nodded. 'You've put it very well.'

'I don't like not making sense.'

'Nor do I.'

'Do we have to go and see this school tomorrow?'

His father didn't answer. His head drooped and he studied his hands for a moment. 'No,' he said at last.

'Thanks, Dad.' Eliot's relief was so immense, he felt light-headed. He read in his father's answer a new beginning, a future where everything was possible. He would see the Morozovs, perhaps very soon, and he would come back to Saintbury, to Noni and Violet, Sam and Nancy Rose. Hope gave him courage and at last he was able to ask, 'Where are the photos of Mum?'

'One is here.' His father reached inside his jacket and brought out a crumpled photograph: Lily standing by a stream, her arms raised and her sunlit hair tumbled by the wind. And there, clutching the string of a silver balloon, was Eliot, in the air.

Eliot smiled but seeing the terrible grief that suddenly claimed his father, he waited until the moment passed and then said gently, 'Shall we walk to Dove Farm now, and I'll tell you about Mary-Ellen?'

The rain had drawn into the air all the wild fragrance of the earth, and now it washed round Eliot and his father as they talked and remembered. And when his father had listened to everything Eliot had to tell about Mary-Ellen Flowers, there remained only one fragment of her story to complete their understanding. So Eliot asked about Gilbert's father, the grandfather he had never known.

'He was a good man,' Gilbert said, 'but solitary and, somehow, lost. I think he would have liked to know who his true parents were, but he was only told that they were dead. He was drowned at sea on Midsummer day, the day I saw *her*, as it happened. I was fifteen.'

Eliot found that he had almost known this. They had turned down the lane to Dove Farm and were enclosed in a tunnel of dripping, glittering leaves. It was easy to imagine light footsteps from the past, just a little way ahead of them.

When they emerged from the lane and stood before the

open gate, Eliot had one last question. 'Didn't they tell your father anything, anything at all about his parents?'

'No.' Gilbert frowned with concentration, and then he said, 'I'm wrong. There was something. They told him his father had won the Victoria Cross for bravery. He was very proud of that.'

Eliot hadn't needed proof, but it was good to have it.

They walked into the cobbled yard, and Gilbert Latimer stared at the ivy-clad farmhouse until his thoughtful gaze was drawn into the shining fields beyond.

'So this is the place,' he murmured.

'What was that?' Fred Bean went to the window. It wasn't a sound that had alerted him. He might have described it as a feeling that ghosts were approaching. An inexplicable shiver. 'Elsie, we've got visitors,' he said.

When he opened the front door they were still there, a man and a boy, standing very close. The man's arm round his son's shoulders. Even the sudden clatter of wings couldn't break their silence or their stillness. The doves fanned out into the deep, midsummer sky and Fred Bean smiled with relief.

'You've come back together, then,' he said.